It Wasn't Fate

BY: William D. Ollivierre

Cover art by: William D. Ollivierre

A MOW Universe Publishing Production
Published by William D. Ollivierre

ISBN: 978-1-7359149-6-1

I would like to thank God for bringing me from a ten-year-old child that could barely read or write, to allowing me to finish and publish book after book.

Also, thank my family and friends for all the support, I wouldn't be writing without it.

Last special thanks to Emoni McGregor for all the help getting this book ready.

For all those who need an escape from reality.
Come escape with me.

Intro

Even if we find a way to control time, faith will always play its part and drive us to where we belong, even against time itself.

These are words spoken by a bleeding heart, stuck on the concept of fate and romance through the ages. They have never met a man determined to control fate. Who will bend time to his will and guide love down the path he sees fit even if it means his complete distraction. Now let's find out who is more powerful, man's never-ending need to control the world around him, defying all the laws of this universe or fate.

Table of Contents

Act 1

Act 2

Act 3

Table of Contents

It Wasn't Fate

IT WASN'T FATE

It's such a beautiful day, the sun is shining brightly, and the wind is blowing a cool breeze across my face. It's the perfect day to tell a story, but it can't just be any kind of story, it must be one that matches this amazing day.

As I think about this beautiful day, only one story comes to my mind. A tale of love, fate, lose and gain. One that will take us far into the past but as close as yesterday. This story beings 500 years ago, but it started only a century ago with one poem.

IT WASN'T FATE

Forever

Flowing through time

Our love will never fade as the ages

Roll by we grow

Evermore in love

Vowing never to let the

Evils around us

Ruin our love.

Act 1

Chapter 1

Five hundred years ago, I spoke the words of that poem to my bride to be on the altar. She was the most beautiful person I had ever seen in my life. I loved her more with each second I spent with her, almost as if I was falling in love with her all over again, every minute of each day I spent with her. My love for her was more than that of the love I had for my own life. And today was the happiest day of my life because from now on it would be the two of us for the rest of our lives.

The words of the poem came from me slowly as if drifting out of my heart into the air as I spoke. My mind was lost as they drifted out, all I could think was my life with her was about to start, and I was going to make sure she was happy with the life we were going to share no matter what it took. She could feel my love and my thoughts as I looked into her eyes speaking the poem, holding onto her hands like my life depended on it.

Everyone in the church stared as I said I do, the love we shared could be seen rippling off of us as she looked back into my eyes and said I do. We were now one, and I felt as if I was the luckiest person in the whole planet, maybe even the universe. Then the words I was waiting to hear for what seemed like a lifetime came. *"I now pronounce you man and wife. You may kiss the bride."*

As the words rang through the church, time stood still for our first kiss as husband and wife.

I looked around the church as we walked down the aisles hand in hand, it was more wonderful than I could have imagined. So many happy faces filled with joy as they watched the two of us, it was as if it were a wonderful dream I would never be waking up from.

We walked into the church separately but were now leaving together as one, this thought filled my mind and my body with warmth. I understood then what it really meant to be in love with someone, to know that I was not alone and would not be alone ever again. This was a feeling I had no words for, it was a feeling so overwhelming that words had not been thought of to express it with any justice. Merely saying that I felt love was not nearly enough, it felt as if such a simple word was an insult to this feeling.

Yet still it got better as I looked over to my new wife and I knew that I was not the only one that was experiencing this overwhelming joy and love. I could feel her heartbeat and the love in each beat as she held my hand, and with each step, we felt as if we were burning, but at the same time, it wasn't hot in the least. This was what I had waited for all my life, to be with the person feeling the love of another and to love them back as much and even more than they loved me.

We entered the car that was waiting for us, and as it pulled away from the church, we looked back at not only the people there waving to us but also the old lives we were now gladly giving up. We were now moving forward on the road of our lives together, and we could only see a beautiful sunrise up ahead on the highway that was our future lives.

We turned to each other as the car moved alone, smiled, and laughed. *"I love you, it feels like a dream. I can hardly believe we are married now."* I said to her, she smiled and held my hand. *"It's not a dream my love."*

Chapter 2

How I long for your sweet embrace once more.

Your touch so soft and tender sending tingles of energy through my skin.

Our lips meet, our bodies tense as we can feel each other's thoughts and wants.

Our embrace grows tight as our lips become inseparable.

Years of love overflow in an instant as we hold each other.

The love between us causes time itself to stop and marvel at us.

Prolonging that instant our lips push fully together.

The moment passes and our lips separate.

Our eyes open and time moves forward to catch up.

Our embrace ends but it's followed by two words.

Our lips move together as all eyes turn to us and the words are spoken for all to hear.

"I do"

IT WASN'T FATE

There I sat waiting to board the plane that we would be taking for our honeymoon, then I remembered there was something I was supposed to do before I left. I had to make a call, it would be to my best friend who wasn't at the wedding, she had been stuck at work and didn't have the time to fly down to attend the wedding.

They called for our group to start boarding. I realize this was the last time I would be able to call her for more than a week. I grabbed my phone out of my bag and headed into the line letting anyone pass me that wanted to. I dialed her as I walked slowly hoping she would pick up before I got to the front of the line. *"Hey Kell I'm at the airport now, the wedding was beautiful you should have been there."* I said speaking quickly as she answered the phone. *"Aw I'm sorry Will, I wanted to be there, but I just couldn't leave work. But I hope you enjoy your honeymoon, I'll see you once you get back right. I should be back by then, well hopefully I will they are starting to talk about staying here longer. I already missed your wedding. I'm so not having fun right now."* Replied Kellie, then I heard my wife's voice. *"Baby come on it's time to get on the plane hurry up."* I waved back to her, so she knew I was coming, then grabbed my bag from the floor, and hurried to the front before they called the last boarded section. *"I'll talk to you later Kell, I have to get going now. I'll call back when we land, and I'll make sure and give you all the details of the wedding next time I call okay Bye."* I said almost dropping my phone as I ran to get onto the plane.

I handed the flight attendant my boarding pass, fumbling around with my phone. I finally caught up to my wife in the plane, she was standing in the aisle where our seat was, waiting for me to get to her. She had saved the window seat for me, I smiled as I kissed her and got into the seat. I looked out the window for a second, then I turn to her as she sat in the seat next to me.

She smiled and gave me a kiss on the cheek, before buckling her seat belt. I smiled as I sat back in my chair, it had been a very long busy and hectic day, but it was so amazing. I relaxed as I looked over at her I could see she was tired. After all, we had both been awake since two in that morning. She was inspecting every detail of everything, while I made sure everything was coming in as planned. Not to mention the hours it took to get ready, well really the hours it took her to get ready, but after seeing her, I knew it was worth it.

I gave her a kiss on the cheek and sat back in my seat buckling my seat belt. *"Baby get some sleep you look tired, I'll wake you up when it's time to land ok."* I said with a smile. *"Ok I will, but you need to get some sleep too you were up before me, and you didn't even sleep the day before."* She said back to me as her eyes closed. I looked at her with her eyes closed, I was tired too, but she was wrong about one thing I hadn't slept for a week, and I didn't think I was going to until we landed that night.

I sat waiting for the plan to take off, it was one of my favorite parts of flying, the moment the plane left the ground and the countdown to when we would be landed begin. I looked at my watch a few more minutes, and it would be six then the plane should be taking off. I looked over at her as the plane's engines turned on, she was already asleep, she must have been more tired than I thought. I looked back out of the window as the plane went down the runway, it turned and the sun was now on my side. I watched as it grew closer and closer to setting then right as the plane lifted from the ground it slowly faded into the ground below. One of the most beautiful sunsets I had seen in my life made only better by the amazing day I just had.

I closed my eyes and managed to drift off to sleep after almost an hour. As I slept, my mind wondered about the day, and what was ahead of me in my new life. Soon my thoughts stopped as I started to dream, this dream was nothing special to most people, but to me it was. It was my first dream in years, well not just years it was my first dream since I was a little child.

In my dream I was sitting on my bed in my new home, it was ten years in the future. I knew I was still happy. However, a lot had changed, as I looked around the room I could see pictures of two children in picture frames all over. I looked at the photos and knew instantly they were mine, they were exactly what I always wanted, twins a boy and a girl. I smiled as I was looking at the pictures, then I felt a tug on one of my legs. I turned to see the two of them holding onto my leg. *"Daddy you promised to take us to the park to..."* My son started to speak, but was interrupted by his sister *"When are we going daddy?"* She said with the biggest smile I had ever seen, all I could do was smile back and take their hands in mine. *"We will go now my little ones, come let's get your shoes, you can't go to the park with no shoes now can you?"* I said to them as we walked out of the room one on each side holding my hand.

Beep. *"Please buckle your seatbelts securely, and put your seats in the upright position. We will be beginning our landing descent shortly."* The pilot's voice said over the intercom waking me from my dream. I looked over and saw my wife sleeping on my shoulder, she must have moved when I was asleep, I smiled and kissed her forehead. *"It's time to wake up baby."* I said softly waking her from her dreams.

The plane landed and we left to get our bags. We watched as all the bags from the plane passed by in front of us on the conveyor. A few minutes passed then it hit me, I had told Kellie I would call her once the plane had landed, I might as well do it now while we were waiting for the bags to come around. I reached into my pocket for my phone, but it was gone. *"Looking for something?"* She said holding my phone in her hand. *"It's our honeymoon, which means no calls to work, no calls from business partners, and no talking to any women that isn't me."* She said with a jealous smile.

Chapter 3

Wake

The Wonderful aroma of your hair fills the

Atmosphere pulling my mind into a world

Kept only for you and me our

Eternal paradise together.

IT WASN'T FATE

I awoke the first morning of our honeymoon, to her face inches away from mine. I smiled it was all I could do. *"It was the first day of the rest of my life."* Was the first thing that came to my mind, I truly understood the meaning of those words now. I kissed her gently so I wouldn't wake her, then I got out of bed carefully.

I walked around the suite we were staying in, I looked over everything making plans for the morning, then headed into the kitchen to see what was there. This was the first day of our marriage and the rest of our life together, it had to be a special day, no it had to be perfect.

I looked through the fridge that was there, not very much to cook with but I wasn't about to let that stop me from making this the day perfect. I went back to the room, and she was still lying in bed sleeping peacefully. Good, I thought. *"I guess not being able to sleep for more than five hours at a time does have its upsides."* I looked over at the clock and grabbed my phone to check the time the sun would be rising, I had just about an hour. It would be more than enough time for me to get breakfast ready. I got dressed quickly and ran out of the room down to the street.

We were staying in Italy, the market was getting ready to open nearby the hotel. I ran to all the vendors that were setting up asking for the ingredients I would need, and any ideas they had that I could make quickly. I glanced at the time I had to start getting things together soon, or I wouldn't have time. I ran to the last vendor all I needed now was eggs. Hopefully, he had eggs the previous three didn't have any, and I was running out of time. He had them, and as I paid for the eggs, my phone started to vibrate. It must be the alarm I had set to remind myself to leave the market, I pulled my phone from my pocket to dismiss the alarm as I ran towards the hotel.

I looked on the screen for the red button, and I saw Kellie's face. I realized I still had a few minutes before the alarm went off as I saw the time. I might as well answer I thought as I answered the call. *"Hey, Kell what's up?"* I said while trying to run and hold everything in my hands at the same time. *"I just got home, and I knew your sweetheart wouldn't be awake yet. It's 5:45 there right? Well anyway, I was just checking in on you, maybe you will have time now to give me some of those details you promised me before you got on the plane, and left me to sleep without anything to think about."* She answered. *"You know it's kind of creepy you know what time it is here when no one was supposed to even know where we were going. If I didn't know any better, I would think you were stocking me."* I said to her laughing. Kellie wasn't just my closest friend she was also my business partner, the one that made sure I stayed on track and finished writing every book I said I was going to. She always knew where I was and what I was doing pretty much all the time. It was like she could read my mind, something I could never figure out how she did, but I didn't really care. *"Well, I don't have the time right now to give you the details of the wedding. I'm in a bit of a rush right now... I'm sorry but I will make sure I tell you everything as soon as possible."* I replied to her, arriving at the entrance to the hotel.

IT WASN'T FATE

I tripped over my feet and almost dropped everything, but somehow I save myself from falling. Pushing the phone back up to my ear all I heard was here laughing. *"You need to be more careful, next time you might actually fall, and then your plans would be ruined."* She said still laughing, I almost asked how she knew but then how could she not after all the noise I just made. *"Well, I know you will tell me when you get back. I only called to see if you were safe, have a good honeymoon. Oh and here's a tip put the eggs in the toaster oven on low and, make sure it's in a glass bowl, it will take 10 minutes to cook so you can watch the sunrise while it does. You're very welcome by the way."* She said as I walked into the door of the hotel. *"Thanks, Kell that will help a lot I'll talk to you soon."* I replied while walking to my room trying to get my key card out. *"Don't worry I know she is going to take your phone, I'll see you when you get back have fun and don't drop the eggs, night."* She said almost laughing. *"Night Kell."* She hung up, and I ended up dropping the phone to save the eggs from falling. That was close I thought. *"It's still weird how she does that."* I said to myself as I reached for my key card and opened the door.

It was still dark in the room, which meant she hadn't woken up yet. I quickly got the eggs ready and placed it in the oven. I had fifteen minutes before the sun would be rising, so I didn't turn it on. I still had a lot to do before I would need to turn it on, and only ten minutes to do it in. I grabbed the flowers I had gotten from the bag, unwrapped them and started separating them into ones. Then used the red ones to draw a line from the room to the table. Then I took the white ones and made a circle around the table. I put the last two bright blue roses in the center of the table and headed to the kitchen to get what I needed to set the table.

I set the table with the white wedding glasses we had gotten the day before, I had managed to hide them in my luggage when she wasn't looking. Then I went to my bag and got the rose I brought with me, one that I had grown myself just for this day. It was blue and pink with just a touch of red in the center, no thorns of any kind, and its smell was like perfume. I had taken great care to twist two of them together as they grew to form what looked like one steam that grew two roses.

I placed it on the table in the center between the other two blue ones. Then I got the flower petals I had brought from the bag and went to the room. I placed them around the bed then made a line leading to the balcony where I spread them to make a red heart with a blue outline. I placed two pillows on the ground behind the heart where we would sit. Three more minutes and the sun would be rising, I had to hurry. I ran back to the kitchen as fast as I could without making any noise. I turned on the oven and the coffee maker then headed back to the room.

"It's time to wake up baby." I said as I kissed her lips, she opened her eyes and pulled me in close for another kiss. She sat up and started to stretch, her face light up as her hands went above her head. Seeing all of the petals around her shocked her and froze her for a moment. *"Aww baby you did this for me that's so cute."* I kissed her again then pulled her from the bed. *"This is just the beginning baby, now hurry*

up and follow the flower petals." We walked to the door, I opened it, and there she saw the blue heart, the red flowers were too dark for her to see at the moment, which was just how I wanted it. Her smile grew even more as we sat. I pointed forward. *"Look baby, it's our first sunrises as a married couple. And it looks like the sun is taking its time just for the two of us today."*

The sunrise was more beautiful than any we had seen before, and it pulled us in as we watched it slowly climb into the sky. The first rays of light hit our faces and as it did the warmth of the light made us feel like the sunrise was just for us and no one else. I leaned over and kissed her lips pulling her attention away from the sun. As I pulled back from the kiss, her eyes saw the heart in front of us again, and she grabbed onto me hugging and kissing me. *"Your amazing baby, I love you so much."* I smiled as I directed her attention to the roses that lead back inside to the table.

I lead her back to the table following the roses on the ground. As she saw the table, her hands flew around me. *"Have I told you how much I love you yet? Where did you find that rose I haven't seen one in years, I thought they stopped making them."* She said as she walked to the table, about to reach for the roses in the middle. *"It's not like the fake one I gave you the first time, that one is real I grew it just for you, just for today. I love you, and I wanted today to be perfect for you."* I said as I walked to the kitchen, by now everything should be hot and ready. I quickly put everything on a tray. Then headed back out to her. She looked up at me smiling as I set the table. *"It's more than perfect baby, you're wonderful. I can't believe you had the time to think of all this and do it."* She said to me as I sat next to her. As we fed each other, I got lost in the moment and started to think about the rest of my life.

The rest of the honeymoon went by like in a flash. We spent the rest of it exploring the city, enjoying the wonderful dinners we made with each other, laughing and joking around. Every day I woke thinking about how lucky I was to be waking up next to her. "***This was all I would need for the rest of my life."*** Was the first thought I had waking up the last day of our honeymoon. It stayed with me all through the flight and left me smiling and happy the whole way.

Chapter 4

A past apart

Now together at last.

Now we embark on a journey

To create new memories.

To go through the good and bad

The up's and downs.

The moments of joy and sorrow

Together we face the future.

Together we create a new past.

IT WASN'T FATE

Our plane landed, and as it did, it marked the end of our honeymoon and our first week together. I walked out of the plane and turned on my phone, as it loaded I got two hundred new emails all from work. Then I got a barrage of text messages and voicemails, once they finally stop coming in, I got one from Kellie. **Hope you enjoyed your week off and your honeymoon. Now it's time to get back to work, you have four articles to finish and three book summaries to review before I send them out tonight, not to mention catching up on all the meetings you missed last week. Oh, by the way I'll be there in ten minutes to pick you up.**

The message snapped me back to the reality of my life as a business owner, I had a lot of work to catch up on for the new year and being gone for a whole week just made it so much worst. As I was opening the emails a hand came over the screen, then it pulled the phone right from my hands. I looked up at my wife. I looked up, and the annoyed look on her face spoke before her words could leave her mouth. *"We just got off the plane, you could at least wait till we get home before you start worrying about work. I do need your attention to you know."* She said with her hands on her hips, looking at me frowning. *"I'm sorry baby, I'll go get the bags while you get a cab for us ok."* I answered then turned and headed to the baggage area.

My wife headed to get a cab, and as she waved for one to stop, a black car pulled up in front of her. *"Hey Crystal how are you, I thought I would come and pick you guys up."* Said Kellie from inside the car as the windows rolled down. *"Really? Well, that's nice of you, even though I know you're just here to get him back to work."* Replayed Crystal with a hint of sarcasm in her voice, as she stepped up to the car and got in the passenger side, then pointed to the door where I would be coming out of. I walked up just as they pulled up in front of the door. The trunk popped open, and I put the bags in as fast as I could, I never liked this airport, everyone here was always in a rush as if they were having the worst day ever.

I finished putting the bags away despite the three cars behind me blowing their horns and the drivers screaming at me to get out of the road, then got into the back seat. I closed the door, and I could feel the tension in the air, Crystal was not happy to see Kellie. ***"She must not want me back at work yet."*** I thought as the car moved forward.

The car ride felt like it was taking forever, five minutes of total silence, not even the radio was on. I looked at the two of them in the front, and I could see the tension between them, I had to do something to break the tension before it got any worst. I opened my mouth to try and say something that would break the tension, but Kellie beat me to it. *"I'm sorry Crystal, but Will has to come back to work today. He has a lot to catch up on that he didn't do because of planning the wedding, and now he has even more to do from being gone a whole week. It's already hard to keep up with everything on my own for a day but a whole week is almost impossible, and I did it so you guys would have a good honeymoon."* Said Kellie, seeming to defuse the tension for a moment, but I didn't know if what she said was going to make it better or make the situation worse.

Crystal just looked over at her very annoyed. *"I know it's hard to do on your own, but I also know they are other people that work for you that can help you out."* Crystal replayed to her not making eye contact for even a moment. *"Yes they are other people that can help me with the work, but he is the face of the publishing aspect of the company, I can send as many emails as I want and make calls all day, but he still has to show up to meetings every once in a while."* Kellie said trying her best not to be annoyed.

Nothing was said for some time after that, so I decided to say something to try and bring peace between the two of them. *"How about this ladies, you both can go out shopping today, I'll deal with the bags, and get all my work done. Then I'll pick you guys back up at eight, then we'll go out to dinner at your favorite restaurant to finish off the day just you baby and me. I know it's not a perfect solution, but you can spend some time together doing something you both like to do. While I do what I have to do, how does that sound?"* I said with my fingers crossed hoping that my idea would go over well with everyone, I did have a lot of work to catch up on and this would give me a chance to do a lot of it, and get the rest in order so I wouldn't be late on anything. *"Okay, I can deal with that today."* Crystal said relaxing a bit and then starting to smile a little. I smiled as I could feel the tension leave the car.

The car pulled up to the house, I got out and took the bags from the trunk then kissed her, she pulled me back as I was about to walk away. *"You better not be late tonight baby."* She said then let me go, I grabbed the bags from the ground and watched as the car drove off. I quickly changed my clothes, got in my car and headed into the office, it was going to be a very long day for me. I would be going from meetings to meetings, and trying to write all my articles in between, and read as many book summaries as possible once I finished the articles.

However, with all I had to do, my mind was somewhere else the whole time, all I could think was how things were going with Crystal and Kellie. It seemed a bit odd to me seeing that they never had a problem before. *"It must just be because we just got back and she isn't ready to let me go back to work just yet."* I said to myself as I headed to one of the meetings.

Chapter 5

Challenges surround us at all ends

Bringing fear of the end

Will our love end

The World pulls us apart

As our hearts cling to one another

We see What the end brings

The pain of loneliness

But love overcomes all

The world pulls with all its power

But this world has no power

Greater than our love.

IT WASN'T FATE

Crystal and Kellie arrived at the mall, and the tension between them seemed to be completely gone, they both had smiles on their faces, with the intention of shopping till they couldn't walk anymore. They were at one of the biggest malls in the state, where Kellie came often but it was the first time Crystal had been there. This was Kellie's favorite place to go when she wanted to relax, she figured bringing Crystal here would help their relationship, seeing that there wasn't another mall as big for almost one hundred miles. Hopefully, she will enjoy herself, then maybe she wouldn't be so hostile towards her all the time, and they could finally all get along. At first, Kellie's plan seemed to be working, but it seemed to be working very slowly.

"So Kellie what do you do when not keeping tabs on my husband." Asked Crystal with a slightly sarcastic attitude, which Kellie did her best to ignore and move on to answering her question. *"Well I don't get all that much time off from work, but when I do I do like to go out, I come here most of the time. I shop, watch a movie, and relax for the whole day sometimes."*

Kellie stopped talking and pulled Crystal into a store. *"This is my favorite store to come to. Whenever I am here I have to come in here even if I don't go to any other store. They sell anything and everything a lady could want to buy, its awesome in here."* Said Kellie excited with a big smile on her face. Crystal looked around the store, and she was right, the store was huge, and it had everything. The walls were filled with cloths of all types and styles, the tables had every kind of makeup and perfume you could think of, and the glass cases in the middle of the store carried the most beautiful jewelry she had ever seen in her life.

As Crystal looked around the store lost in where to start a salesman walked up to them, with a smile and bowed slightly, something that caught Crystal a bit off guard. *"Hello Miss Kellie how are you doing today, I see you're with a friend today. Are you going to introduce me to her?"* He said as he turned to Crystal taking her hand and kissing it softly before he let go. *"Of course I am, John. This is Crystal, she is Will's' new wife. They just got back from their honeymoon today, and I thought I would bring her here to get her a proper wedding gift."* Kellie answered as John smiled. *"Well then, you brought her to the right place..."* Said John as he walked around Crystal looking her over from top to bottom.

"I Hope your ready Crystal because this guy is like magic, he always knows just what I need to make my day. This is how I stay so happy even with keeping track of your husband and him forgetting things and making so many people angry at work." John looked at them smiling. *"Oh stop I'm not magic, but I do know exactly what will make your day today, follow me ladies."* John said walking towards the back of the store, as they followed John, Crystal wondered what they were going to get. Looking around at everything the store carried as she walked surprised her, and the share size of the place was stunning.

"Kellie I don't see that many people that work here, are they all helping people like he is helping us or are we special." Crystal said looking back at Kellie. Kellie Smiled it seemed as though her plan was starting to work. *"No, your right we are special, our company has an*

account here we get everything we need for the models that do the book covers here, we also take the cover shots for all the authors that we publish here. That and we featured them in a lot of the work we do. So every time I come in here, they are always happy to see me, that and I do shop a lot." Replied Kellie, as she walked behind curtains that blocked off the back of the store.

"Oh, I did forget to tell you this place has the best spa in the state." Kellie said with a smile as Crystal looked around the back of the store, then back at her with a smile. Kellie's plan had worked, the tension between the two was all gone. "Well are you just going to stand there looking around, I thought you two wanted to relax?" The voice of John said as he walked up with two robes. "No we aren't just going to stand here, we are going to have fun right Crystal?" Kellie said taking the robes from John and pulling crystal off to the dressing room. "You know Kellie, I'm kind of jealous of how much time you get to spend with Will, I mean he is my husband now, but you know where he is more than I do. I'm not upset with you or anything I just want to know how you do it, and I want him home more often." Crystal said to Kellie while they changed.

"Well Will is not the kind of person you can control, he is a workaholic a lot of times. However, he is a simple person, he always follows his patterns, that and his phone updates where he is every time he stays in one place for more than five minutes. He is also horrible with directions meaning his GPS is always on, which you should know by now. That's how I can keep up with him leaving all the time. That and *his personal email and calendar accounts are synced to mine so I can make sure he doesn't ignore important emails or miss meetings."* Said Kellie, which didn't really go well for keeping things good between the two but she managed to save herself. *"Don't worry I'll show you how to sync your stuff too. After we leave here that is. For now, let's just enjoy the rest of the day and get you ready for your date tonight."* She said smiling.

Chapter 6

As the days and nights pass by our love grows

slowly falling deeper and deeper

into the ocean known as love.

Pulled deeper into its depths

By the ever-strengthening hands of time.

We surrender and let it's warmth fill our beings

This is love this is life this is ours.

IT WASN'T FATE

Whatever Kellie did worked amazingly, was all I could think as I saw them walking up to me laughing and talking. They looked as if they had been best friends for years, and as they got closer, I saw what they were wearing, and it was stunning. They both looked beautiful in their new dresses. *"Hey, baby I'm ready for our date now. Oh did you manage to catch up on the work you wanted to do today."* Crystal asked then kissed me on the cheek leaving me speechless for a few seconds. *"It was a good day baby I managed to finish all my articles, well the ones that were due today anyway, and I even had time to read all the summaries that needed to be sent out tonight. Just have to go to a few meetings tomorrow and I'll have nothing overdue from last week. You look amazing by the way."* I said with a smile.

We got into the car, and I drove off, I had made reservations at one of my favorite high-class restaurants that was almost impossible to get a reservation at. I was hoping to surprise her and get her to relax about work more. It was a very strange car ride, she was just sitting next to me clinging to my arm as I drove talking about work. Something I found bizarre after her big argument this morning about me liking work too much. The whole car ride was one question after the next, she asked about what I did today, what I was planning for the next day, and what I was planning in general for the company. Even though I thought it was very nice she was getting interested in my work, it seems very odd that it happened all of a sudden. But I paid the strange feeling no mind as I answered her questions, it wasn't that important at the moment whether or not she was interested in what I was doing at work.

The car ride lasted fifteen minutes, and all I did was answer her questions the entire time. Which I had to admit was actually very enjoyable, and insightful making me see just how much stuff I actually did at work. I smiled as we pulled up to the restaurant, I handed the valet the key and opened the door for her, as I wondered what she did with Kellie today that brought on all those questions.

As we sat at our table, I looked up at her and could tell she was enjoying herself. At that moment it was as if a switch of joy went off in both of us. We talked and laughed like never before as we waited for the waiter to bring our order. Then as I looked up at her as she ate she seem to glow, it was as if the sun was rising behind her. I smiled while staring at her making her blush, which made me feel as if everything in the entire room was suddenly now glowing. I sat back in my chair smiling and continued our conversation from before. Every minute of the dinner seemed to just melt away, and before we knew it, it was already closing in time.

We left the dinner happier than we had been since we met, we had no worries of any kind, and the feeling that things are going to be perfect from this moment on filled both of us. The night got even more amazing as we headed back to our home for the first time. We walked into a new house for the first time hand-in-hand. This would be where we would spend the rest of our lives, I thought to myself. This our new home was made even more fitting for us, because we had both sold the houses we lived in before to buy this one.

IT WASN'T FATE

We laid together in the living room making plans for our new home, talking about the lives we used to have, and talking about the life we were going to have now.

That night was a truly an amazing night, and it felt as if it would never come to an end just extending on forever.

Chapter 7

Change

We have started to change

Change is a wonderful thing

We must keep moving forward

Keep changing

Never stop, never give up

Hold fast for this is only the beginning

IT WASN'T FATE

The days passed us by quickly. Soon turning into weeks then months, and as the time passed, we grew. Our lives changed, some of it was for the better, and some things were just changes.

At first, we grew closer to one another, we did everything together, but then we started to grow apart. Well, that's what she said this morning before I left for work. So here I am now, thinking back over the past six months of my life, well our lives. *"Does she not understand that I have to work, I can't always be home with her... and it's not like she is home alone any way she has her friends over all the time and she goes out to."* I said to Kellie as she sat across from me reading an article I had written the night before. *"Well maybe she just wants you home a little more, or she wants you to pay more attention to her when you are home, instead of doing things for work."* Replied Kellie without once looking up from the paper in her hand.

I thought for a while then responded when she looked up from the paper in front of her. *"Well I do pay attention to her, I give her all the time she wants when I'm home. But she acts like I'm not going to work and just leaving the house so that I can get away from her. I don't know what to do, or say to her to make things better anymore."* Kellie looked at me, then slightly back down at the paper, I could tell she knew something I didn't.

"What aren't you telling me Kellie and don't try to lie to me, you know I can tell when you're lying so just tell me." I said, as I looked her in the eyes. *"Oh fine fine, I'll tell you, but you can't let her know that I told*

you okay." I just nodded as she continued to talk. *"Well remember the first day me and her went out, well I kinda sorta gave her the passkey to your calendar. The one I use to know where you are all the time and make sure you get your work done."* She said while avoiding looking me in the eyes.

"You do know the passkey for that unlocks all my accounts also don't you, and you do realize that a lot of my accounts are linked into yours?" She looked back at me with an annoyed look of guilt. *"Yes, I know that. I was the one that got you to set it up that way. I only gave it to her so she would know you were at work and not just out doing something else."* She responded to me still looking down, I sighed and continued to talk. *"That explains why she doesn't like you so much now. I always thought it was because you knew me better than she does, but now I know it's because of how much time we spend together. I know you never used it, but there is a meeting function that records any two people in a room as being in a meeting. It also has a total button that totals the amount of time I spend in meetings with each person over the month. I set it up so I would remember to make time for all of my clients, and bill the ones that took up more time than necessary. But if she found it and used it on you then she would realize that I spend all the time at work with you, now do you see how that was a bad idea?"* I said to her with a hint of the distress in my voice.

Kellie looked at me realizing what would most likely be going through Crystal's mind, then she got up. *"Well that might be a problem, you're going to have to find a way to make her feel better about things.*

And you better do it soon because I have a feeling it will be affecting the company too." She said as she headed for the door and looked at me to follow.

We had a list of meetings set up for that day that seems to have no end, not only that but they started so close to each other that I would have no time to do anything else but run from one meeting room to the next all day. Which meant this would be another day that the calendar would show me and Kellie spending the entire day together in a meeting.

At the end of the day I was exhausted, I felt as if I had been running around the entire day nonstop. I didn't even have time to take a break for a snack. As the final meeting finished, I darted out of the door straight for my car. I headed straight home hoping there wouldn't be too much traffic that day.

I got home that afternoon, and as I walked in I saw Crystal sitting at the dining table, I walked into the door, and she looked at me. *"So how was your big day of meetings, must have been pretty busy not to have any time to call me right."* She said as she watched me closely as if she was looking for something on my clothes. *"Babe I know you know I was in meetings all day, Kellie told me about giving you the passkey so I know that you could see who I was in meetings with all day."* I replied as calmly and as nicely as I could.

"So I guess you're going to try and say I'm spying on you now right, well I wouldn't have to if it wasn't for her. You know I see how she is always with you and never has a boyfriend, I know what she's doing." I

sighed as I took my shoes off and sat in the couch across from her, this was just what I was afraid would happen. *"What! You have nothing to say now, is that it, maybe you like the attention from her."* She yelled as I pulled my other shoe off. My head was hurting now, I began to stand to my feet as I talked. *"Babe its, its um its…"* My words were cut short as the pain shot through my head like a bolt of lightning, then everything was just darkness.

Act 2

Chapter 1

The word love

Love so true and pure

Overwhelming in its beauty

Virtuous, strong and, unbreakable

Everlasting through the ages.

IT WASN'T FATE

I woke up in a hospital room hooked up to all kinds of machines. My vision was blurred, and my eyes burned as I looked around. My eyes slowly adjusted to the light in the room and the burning sensation in my eyes was replaced by a throbbing, stabbing pain behind my left eye. I tried to sit up, but the pain shot through my whole body in an instant and froze my body. *"Don't move Will, the doctors said when you wake up it will take some time before you are strong enough to do anything. Just relax and try to rest."* Said a woman's voice I didn't recognize, then before my eyes fully cleared up I heard another voice. *"He shouldn't be awake just yet, I'll give him something for the pain, and to make him go back to sleep, call me the next time he is awake."* It must be the nurse I thought, but whatever she gave me kicked in and I was out before I could even finish my thought.

"Hey Will come on, wake up now." I heard the voice again, I still didn't know who it was but why did it sound like they knew me. I opened my eyes the pain was less than before but it wasn't gone, my eyes quickly cleared up, and I could see clearly again. Everything was very bright, then I unknowingly turned my head towards the window. The bright light from outside made me closes my eyes quickly before I could see who was in the room with me. *"Relax Will I'll close the blinds, I still don't get how you can dislike sunlight so much when it makes everything better."* The person said as I heard them close the blinds, what they said only proved to me that they knew me personally but who was it. I opened back my eyes, as it cleared up, I saw her sitting

there. *"Kellie is that you?"* I said slowly struggling to get the words out.

"Yes, Will it's me, who else would it be…" Her face suddenly changed to one of fear. *"Don't tell me you can't see me, they said this might happen, but the doctors said it would most likely be temporary."* She said trying her best to hide the panic in her voice.

"Relax I can see you just fine but you sound so different how long have I been in here, it couldn't be that long right?" She looked at me still with a panicked face then looked down. *"Actually it has been a long time."* She said as she put her face down into her hands then all she said was. *"Ten"* My eyes dropped, I was shocked I had been here for ten years. *"Ten, ten years what happened to me why I was here that long. And what happened to our business and Crystal."* I was panicking on the brink of tears, she jumped up from the chair. *"Relax Will it's only been ten days not years everything is still ok. You had a stroke. They said that it was on the nerves that affect your vision. Try and relax the doctor said you're going to be ok they ran a lot of tests to see if they can find out what was the cause."* She said with a hint of sadness.

I looked at her with some relief, then around the room. *"Kellie where's Crystal?"* I asked her as I looked around the room. *"She's at home, she doesn't really know how to handle being in hospitals. I've been here trying to run things from your computer while I waited for you to wake up."* She said as I could see the disappointment on my face, as the thoughts flowed through my mind. Why wasn't she here for me, was it because of the fight, or was it something else. *"Stop thinking already your brain is still recovering from a stroke you know. She said* she doesn't do well in hospitals, so just leave it at that. Be happy I was here with you the whole time, you know I actually overheard one of the nurses say that I was your mistress, can you believe that…" Her voice faded out as I lost consciousness.

"Wake up Will, come on I don't like being here watching you sleep like this." I opened my eyes, and she was right there over me. "Well do you recognize my voice this time, now that you're off of all the painkillers?" Said Kellie, I looked up at her then sat up as she sat in the chair next to the bed. "Well yes and no, I recognize it, but for some reason it sounds different, well for that matter everything kind of sounds a bit off." I replied to her. "Well, it must be because you were asleep for so long. Don't worry about it now anyway." She said back to me with a smile.

"The doctors gave me the ok for you to go home and back to work, as long as you took things easy from now on and didn't stress things as much as you did before." But that wasn't all Kellie told me. "Well I wanted to tell you this myself before any of the nurses had a chance to, so I stayed with you until you woke up. The doctors said that your stroke was caused by something you already had." She paused and got up and closed the door, then walking back she sat on the side of my bed. "Will you have MS, They said that you're going to have to go through treatment for a few weeks to get it under control before you will be able to walk again." My eyes were wide when I heard the last words. "What do you mean walk again?" I said as I looked down to my feet. "They said that after the stroke you had what's called a flare-up, it's where the *nerves in your brain get damaged by your immune system. This time it was the nerves that control the lower half of your body that were affecting."* She said calmly and slowly.

She must be kidding I thought, I could feel my feet just fine, I could even feel her leaning on them gently. Then I tried to move them but nothing, she looked at me and nodded she could tell that I was figuring it out, but the look on her face said this wasn't the first tie she saw me do this. *"The first time you woke up you tried to get out of bed and started screaming your legs are missing. They had to put you back to sleep."* She said to me as she leaned back in her chair.

"So how I am going to go home if I can't walk, this doesn't make sense." I said panicking. She looked at me and spoke as there was a knock on the door. *"Well you're going to be in a wheelchair for a while, that must be the nurse now to get you ready to leave."* She said heading towards the door to open it. *"Hello my name is the Nafisa, I'm your nurse, and I'll help you get ready to leave okay."* The nurse said as she wrote on my chart, and started to remove all the things connected to my body.

A few hours later and I was finally leaving the hospital, Kellie spent most of the time I was getting ready on the phone, so I'm guessing she called Crystal already. She handed me the phone and pushed the wheelchair out of the room. *"I am so ready to get out of here, I've had enough of being in hospitals for a long time."* Kellie said as she walked down the halls to the exit. *"What do you mean you have had enough, I am the one that was sick you know."* I said looking back at her pushing me. *"Hey hey don't you start with me, I'm the one that has been sitting in that room the whole time you were out cold."* She said to me sounding a little bit annoyed, I looked back at her again this time with a small smile. *"Thank you for being there I'm sorry, so is Crystal coming to pick us up so you can go home."* I said waiting for a yes. I knew she would come to get me after all she had been home the whole time she won't be too tired to get us.

"No she isn't coming to get us, but its ok your brother should be outside, he took the day off from work to make sure you got home. I think his wife is coming too, but we will see soon." It made me sad that she didn't come after not staying with me in the hospital, but someone came. My brother and his wife had come to get me, Kellie helped me into the car then sat next to me. *"Relax Will don't worry about anything right now everything will be ok."* She said with a smile as the car drove off.

The drive from the hospital to my house was about half an hour, but it felt like hours as I sat and thought about what had just happened to me. I wondered what I would do next, I wondered if I would ever walk again, and I wondered if things between Crystal and me were going to be okay. I knew my life was going to be different from this point on, but I didn't realize how different it was going to be.

Finally, the car pulled into my driveway I was home, all my thoughts faded away, there was only one thought left. I was scared of what was to come. That thought was if Crystal would be there when I opened the door.

Chapter 2

It took it

I see many pictures

The person is always smiling

Looking so happy no care in the world

An Innocent kind and caring face

Who is this person in these pictures?

I do not recognize the face

Yet somehow, I know it

I think for hours who is this?

Finally, I ask who this person is

The question seems to shock everyone

Who is it, why won't they tell me?

They look at me and speak slow and low

It is you.

Don't you remember?

My mouth speaks without me know

Of course, how could I forget I was kidding.

One thought comes to my mind

The darkness has taken something else from me.

IT WASN'T FATE

It wasn't ok after all, I got home, and Crystal looked at me and then just walked away, not one word was spoken to me. I looked down at the bump at the door then tried to get over it. My hands were not as strong as they use to be. I closed my eyes then the chair moved shocking me, I opened my eyes and looked back. *"She's just shocked give her some time it will all go back to normal just wait and see."* Said Kellie, as she pushed me into the house, she smiled, but it was a lie I could tell she was just trying to make me feel better.

That night was a silent one as me and Crystal laid in bed, not a single word was said between us. Soon my mind began to wonder. Was she was mad, or maybe she just didn't know what to say to me, well maybe she felt guilty about the fight we had when it happened. But I didn't really care much about the reason, just that she wasn't saying a single word to me at all, not even a good night.

The next day came, and I was sure things would start to get better but I was wrong, she didn't say anything at all to me not even good morning. But I didn't get mad about it instead I just tried to talk to her. But she still wouldn't speak, at times she would nod her head but never a single word. I tried day after day to get her to talk to me about what was going on, but after a week I just couldn't anymore, I gave up trying to get through to her. Then another week passed by and I started to learn how to do my daily task on my own. I stopped asking her to help me, and soon it was as if she wasn't even in the house with me. The sound of the wheels of my chair squeaked in the house as I moved around every morning, but they were no voices or footsteps.

I quickly fell into a downward spiral and began to push everyone

45

else away, without Crystal talking to me I felt like I was rejected, and I began to push everyone else away that was trying to help me. Before long me and Kellie were fighting every day over everything at work, which meant business was not doing great. After a week of fighting with Kellie and complete silence at home, I was going crazy and just wanted my old life back the way it was before everything happened. Soon I just shut down and lost track of everything, I just lived day to day like nothing mattered. I was stuck in my mind, and not even my life mattered anymore.

Then it happened. *"I think we need space to think about us."* Said Crystal one night out of the blue about two months after we had stopped talking. *"Space! Space! What more space do you need, we haven't talked in two months what more space is there."* I said exploding out. *"I think we need to be apart for a while, have some time away from each other to think, you know."* She responded to me in a bleak almost cold-hearted tone of voice. *"No, I don't know. What more space could you possibly want, I mean do you want me on the moon, would that finally be enough for you then."* I said angrily as I rolled to the edge of the bed, she didn't respond this time she just sat on the bed looking down. My mind was filled with angry and so much sadness that I couldn't say anything else. I just reach for my cane and pulled myself up off the bed.

That was the last straw, I snapped and lost my hold on reality that night. I went downstairs and laid on the couch looking at the ceiling my eyes filling with tears running down my cheeks. Then out of nowhere, he walked up. *"See I told you she didn't love you, like anyone could ever love someone like you, your already broken."* The words he said hit me hard, so hard that I forgot that I was in my house and there was a strange man in my living room telling me how worthless I was. As the tears rolled down my cheeks, he walked over to me, he shook his head, as reality slowly crept back into my brain, I started to realize what was going on.

"Wait where did you come from, and how did you get in here. You don't even know me so how are you telling me about myself." I responded reaching for my cane. *"Now get out of my house before I call the cops!"* I yelled picking up my cane getting ready to swing it at him, but he just looked at me with a smug smile then started laughing. *"What are you going to do with that thing, do you really think there is anything you can do with that stick."* He said laughing louder than before mocking me.

My anger grew even more, I griped my cane tightly with both hands. *"Get out of my house!"* I yelled out then swung my cane as hard as I could right for him. I was going to make him leave, whether it was willingly or if I had to force him out of my house. My cane flew through the air straight for his body I bet he wished he had left now I thought.

Then I fell from the couch as my cane went straight through what was supposed to be his waste. I hit the carpet hard. I was stunned more than I was hurt by the fact that my cane went straight through him. He walked closer to me then looked at me with an evil smile that stretched from ear to ear. *"Man I can't believe you did that, I mean seriously don't* you recognize me." I looked up at him angry and confused. Wondering what was going on, and what he meant by don't I recognize him. I had never seen him in my life I was sure of that fact. He leaned over so I could see his face more clearly and his smile grew airier.

It hit me like a brick wall he was on the cover of one of my books, I didn't recognize him at first but he was the face of my heroes, I had spent months doing drawings of him with Kellie. He pulled back and stood up then started to talk. *"I see you finally realize who I am now."* The expression on my face change to one of horror as I pulled myself back up onto the couch and he patted me on the shoulder. Was this a crazy fan that broke into my house or was it something worse, someone that wanted me dead maybe.

"No you're not dreaming Will, you of all people should know, that you're having a psychotic break right now, and don't go asking me a dumb question like how you know this is all in your head." He said as he walked around the couch.

"This has to be a dream it must be one, there is just no way this is really happening to me right now..." My words were interrupted. *"Will, who are you talking to?"* Crystal's voice said in horror, her voice caught me by surprise shocking me back into reality. The next second he was gone, my mouth opened to speak but all I could do was stutter on my words in silence. *"I'm going to stay with my mom for a while, I don't know how to deal with this right now."* She said as she pulling her bag over her shoulder at the top of the stairs. She rushed down the stairs then out the door before I could even open my mouth. I didn't even move before she closed the door behind her.

Chapter 3

My heart longs for you

Day and night

I await your love

To save me

To make me what I should be

To complete me.

IT WASN'T FATE

The days in my house passed by slowly as my friend returned to keep me company daily, and even bringing friends with him from time to time. The odd thing was that he was the only thing that kept me from killing myself. But I guessed that would be expected, after all, if I died he died to so why wouldn't he try to keep me from killing myself. Not just that but, it seemed as though his whole point in existing was just to make me miserable and make sure I stayed alive, it was a pretty good way of doing that. Which also meant that, he did his best to help me push everyone around me away.

But it was when I finally gave him a name that things really changed, from that point on my mental state took a nose dive off the deep end. It wasn't long before I stopped talking to any real people outside of work, and even at work I said very little, I only spoke when I had to. I closed myself off from the real world, but still, a part of me wanted to reach out to someone, I just didn't know how to or even what I would say if I managed to find someone to talk to.

The time passed as I grew worst, soon I lost track of the days and began missing work, I was lost in my own world stuck in my head. *"Ok, you need to get some help from someone now."* Said Phil that was what I had named him after a few weeks of seeing him. I turned back to him. *"What do you know about what I need to do, and I thought you didn't care."* I yelled at him, he just walked around me looking me up and down from head to toe. *"Well, I don't actually care about you. I just care that you're alive and at this rate it doesn't look like you will be lasting*

50

much longer, so you're going to get help, and you're not going to die because if you die I die, and that's not happening any time soon if I have anything to say about with it." He said with a serious look on his face, much like the look on the covers of my books.

After that, he left, and I didn't see or hear anything from him for two weeks until everything changed. I walked into my office and sat at my desk across from Kellie and started working on one of my articles, all that was heard was the sound of my fingers hitting the keys on the keyboard. About ten minutes into writing my article, I saw him standing there behind Kellie with an evil smirk on his face, but I ignored him thinking maybe he would go away if I did. *"Oh come on, I know you see me."* He said and walked around her gliding his hand on her shoulders. Then through her hair, I knew he was just trying to get my attention, but knowing what he was trying to do didn't stop it from working. **"What do you want, why did you come back?** I yelled out in my mind, but he just put his hand to his ears acting like he couldn't hear me. I yelled out in my mind louder and louder, but he kept it up every time.

Finally, I opened my mouth to say it aloud, but suddenly I chocked, then what came out shocked me. *"Please Kellie I need help, I don't know what to do anymore."* Kellie looked up shocked by what I just said, but at the same time, she looked relieved by what I had said. He smiled behind her, with a smile of success. *"Well my work here is done I'll be seeing you around, and don't think you will ever be able to get rid of me."* He said winking as he disappeared, I realized then that Kellie was no longer sitting in the chair across from me but was standing next to me with her hand out. *"Come on I'm taking you to see a doctor, I'm so happy you're ready to get better everything will be ok now don't worry."* She said taking my hand.

But sadly, this wasn't true well I didn't think it was true anyway. The last words Phil had said echoed through my mind from that point on, like an ominous warning.

I spent the next week in a mental hospital getting treatment. Which for the most part meant talking about everything that went wrong in my life and taking pills. The whole week seemed to drag on forever, but at the same time, it felt as though I was getting better, which made me feel better as I thought about it. After a week, they decided that I was not a danger to myself though I still needed to take the pills they gave me. So I was sent home, but I wasn't to go back to work for another week. I had to relax and take it easy, and not get stressed about anything, to let my mind process everything that had happened to me away from the stress of my normal life.

So I did just what I was told to do, I went home I took my pills, I turned everything off, and just laid swinging in my hammock looking at the plants and birds in my backyard. Then I watched the sunset for the first time since Crystal left, as the last rays of the sun peaked over the horizon I let everything I was thinking float out of my mind. I did this every day for a week, I awoke and watch the sunrise, I went to the park and enjoyed nature around me, the people, animals, and trees. Halfway through the week, I felt so different, my mind had finally started to cope with everything that had happened to me, and I felt as if I was getting better finally.

Kellie came and took me back to the doctors for them to see if I could go back to work at the end of the week, and they said it would be good for me to start going back to work one day at a time. It would get me back into the life I had before all this happened, and even though I didn't want to go back to work just yet, I thought it would be a good idea to go and get out of the house more.

Chapter 4

Lives once together now apart

Lives once apart now together

That which was alone is joined

That which was joined separated

Change waits but for none.

IT WASN'T FATE

Work was a bit different from what I thought it was going to be, but it was what I needed. A few days of going to work, and staying home passed by, and I decided that I needed to do a bit more to get back to my old self. So I asked Kellie to find me somewhere fun to go where I could relax and enjoy my day, and spend some time writing. I sat back with my eyes closed as she looked for someplace for me to go, I hadn't gone out or taken a trip for fun in almost a year, matter of fact the last time was on my honeymoon with crystal.

She sent me to an arcade for the rest of the afternoon, she said she would pick me up after and tell me what we were going to do after. Kellie took me to watch a movie then out to dinner with a few of her friends that night when she picked me up. Being around people who weren't a part of all the things that had gone wrong in my life as of late was good for me. Actually, it was more than good, I felt better than I had felt in a very long time. I was finally starting to get back to myself that night, as I picked up a piece of paper and started jotting down notes for a new book.

The next two weeks passed by much easier and faster than I expected, I was starting to get back to myself fully. I was smiling laughing and beginning to enjoy my days for the first time since I left the hospital when this all started. I even managed to work up enough courage, to plan a trip to go see Crystal. Maybe I would be able to talk to her about what happened, hopefully even find out the real reason she wanted time to herself, and what was going on inside her head.

IT WASN'T FATE

I decided that I would go that weekend, as the time grew closer, I grew more determined. The Saturday morning I woke up feeling like a completely new person ready to go, much like I used to feel every day. With this newfound determination, I even decided to make the two-hour drive by myself.

I pulled out of the driveway slowly, then headed off out onto the highway driving as slowly and as carefully as traffic would allow me to. And after half an hour of driving, the GPS still said two hours left something I wasn't too concerned about seeing it was still early in the morning. But then it happened.

"Hey there Mr. Will." A voice said from the passenger seat. The voice shocked me, but at the same time, it was so familiar that I didn't even have to turn to know who it was. *"Phil, what are you doing here?"* I said to him as I gripped the steering wheel. He laughed for a little while then started talking. *"Didn't I tell you I would be back, well I know I didn't exactly say that, but I did tell you can't get rid of me."* His voice was more confident than I had ever heard before to the point where I could almost feel it inside of me. I took a quick glance over at him, and he looked nothing like before, he was no longer the character from the cover of my book. His hair was different, his clothes had changed, his eye color had changed, and he was taller and better built. The only thing about him that was the same as before was his voice.

He looked over at me with a smile. *"How do you like my new look, I've been working out a little."* He said cracking his fingers against the dashboard of the car. *"I do have to admit you have changed quite a bit,*

56

but how did you change this much. You look nothing like I envisioned any of my characters. I can't even say I would've ever thought up this look for you." I said while slowing down. *"Come on I thought you were going somewhere, why are you slowing down so much, even that old lady over there is getting mad at you right now."* He said pointing out of the window to the left of me.

I turned to see an old lady waving at me and yelling. *"How did you..."* I started to say before I was cut off. *"Haha, I'm not the same person, thing or whatever you want to call me anymore. I'm a whole new person. Oh yeah by the way my name isn't Phil anymore its Peter now."* He said to me, seeming to almost dare me to defy what he was saying. I was left speechless by his whole new demeanor. *"Come on now you have to get going. It's not like this is the first time you've seen me, and it won't be the last time like I said before. But for now, I have something more important to attend to."* He said to me than just vanished from the seat.

He left me quite a bit shaken up, but mostly confuses to what he meant by he had something more important to do. My mind kept going over those words over and over again as I drove. I wondered what could possibly be going on in my head that I thought I was getting better when I might be getting worse. After a half an hour of these thoughts running through my head, I couldn't take it anymore and I pulled over.

"No you don't, you better get back on that road, and you better start driving like a normal person and get to the house already." The voice of Peter said out of nowhere. I turned and looked to the

passenger seat but he wasn't there, I sighed with relief as I turned back to face the road. There he was standing on my dashboard a few inches tall. I was at a loss for words, but it didn't really matter seeing that he had already started yelling again. *"You have no reason why you should be stopping right now. You spent all this time fighting me, and now you're giving up. I thought you said those doctors were making you better, but from what I can tell they're only making you into someone you're not. Now you get back on the road and try to get there sometime soon. After all my job is already done, you are alive, and you don't want to die anymore."* The tiny Peter said to me.

His words might have been exactly what I needed at that moment, I switched the car back in gear and sped onto the highway. Within an hour I was pulling into the city where Crystal's mother's house was.

I pulled up to the driveway soon after, and as I did my hands froze to the steering wheel. All the determination I had when I left was completely gone from me the instant I saw a shadow in the window that looked like crystal. I pulled myself together as best as I could and pulled into the driveway slowly.

I got out of the car and walked towards the front door. Time around me seem to almost stop as my nervousness grew with each passing second. I rang the doorbell and waited for what seemed like an eternity, then after I didn't hear a reply or footsteps heading to the door, I went to turn to leave. *"Wait don't go I'm coming just hold on a second."* Said a voice from behind the door, I couldn't tell if it was Crystal or her mother, but as I heard the voice my heart stopped. Then I heard the first footstep, and my heart skipped another beat.

Thoughts started racing through my mind, I didn't think I would be able to do this I had to go, and I had to go now. I turned to walk away from the door then I heard the door start to open it was too late for me to leave. I turned back to the door quickly and brace myself to see who it was, the door swung open slowly and there standing behind the door was Crystal.

Chapter 5

Time once on my side

Has betrayed me

It has turned on me

It slows to prolong my pain

It speeds to keep us apart.

IT WASN'T FATE

There I stood speechless as I stared at her, all the thoughts of what I was going to say when I saw her, were all gone and my mind went blank. Time had slowed to a crawl around us, as neither of us knew what to say. It felt like we were both just standing at the door for hours before anything happened. *"Who is it crystal?"* Said a female voice from inside the house, which I assumed was her mother. A few seconds passed before crystal answered. *"Its ok mom I'll be right back ok."* She said snapping both of us back to regular time.

She pulled the door close behind her and started walking to the bench at the side of the house. My heart raced as I followed her to the chair and sat next to her. The next few minutes were spent in silenced that felt like hours as we both searched for words to say to each other.

"Why did you come here?" She said breaking the silence. As happy as I was for the silence to be broken I wished it was other words that broke it. *"Well I haven't seen you in months, and I miss you, I wanted to see how you were doing."* I replied softly almost unheard. She looked at me, but at the same time, it was like she didn't want to look at me. I couldn't tell if it was because she didn't want to see me or if she just didn't know what to say to me. *"I just wanted to know if we could talk for a little while and try to figure things out."* I said hoping for a reply, but it stayed silent.

"Well can you at least tell me what happened? Why did you move out?" I said breaking the silence after a few minutes of waiting for an answer. She looked over at me, I could see that there was something

wrong with her.

"Will how long have we known each other, just think about it for a while." She replied to me with a voice holding back from crying. "Well I'm not sure, but it's been more than ten years since I first said hi to you." I said back to her wondering what that had to do with anything, to me that was even more reason for her to not leave. "Exactly, and what have I called you all this time since we met?" I paused to think about what she had asked, it wasn't a question I fully understood, and she could see it in my confused face.

"Oh how I love you, my Superman. But now I don't know what to do about things." She said, the words snapping back memories and something I had said a long time ago when we first met. Was that the reason, because I said I would always be her Superman, but it couldn't be the reason everything had changed.

"I see you remember now, well it's not the reason I wanted to have some space, but it did help me make the choice. From the time we met you have always been the person that will never stop living up to everything you have ever said, and more, doing it all as if it was nothing. But I never knew just how much you really worked because it always seemed like you were there with me whenever I wanted you to be. But after we got back from our honeymoon I saw just how much you worked, day and night you were working. You weren't even at your office, but yet still you were working, something I have never seen anyone do with so much ease. It's as if your work is who you are and without it, you're not the same person." She said to me looking down at

62

my hands and taking one and turning it over then running her fingers over my palm gently.

"But I made time for you every day and night more than I did before we were married, so I don't understand what the big deal is." I said back to her looking at her face as she kept her head lower to prevent herself from making eye contact with me. A few minutes passed by in silence as she just stared at my hands.

"It's not about the time that was never the issue, from the time we met you were always thinking what would be next after you got what you were just starting to work towards. You never had a goal for your life you just have steps to a goal I never even knew, and a part of me still thinks that you have no goal that will make you happy. But I didn't care as long as I was in your life it would be enough for me, or so I thought... Day after day I watched you go to work and spend all day with that woman, but I accepted it because it was for work and you never let it get between us. But I couldn't just stand by and watch forever. So I decided I was going to change things between us. But everything changed in a way I would have never expected it to. That day you came home, I was determined to changed things somehow, but for some reason, I didn't know what I was going to say to you. By the time you got home, I had been thinking about it and looking at your calendar seeing you were in a meeting with her all day, and I just got angry... You got home, and I was ready for you, then it all changed, you hit the ground, and I panicked I had never once expected you to be sick. After all, you were my Superman. You laid on the ground, I didn't know what to do to help you. I am a doctor, and I was frozen staring at you on the ground hardly breathing. Even when the ambulance came to get you I didn't know what to do, I couldn't even go with you to the hospital I was so shocked." She said to me, and I could tell that there were tears in her eyes as she spoke.

"It's okay, anyone would be scared if that happened to someone they love." I said trying to reassure her to stop her crying. She glanced up at me for a moment then back down, then she let go of my hand and continue to speak.

"That's not the worst part. When you were in the hospital I didn't want to do anything, I just sat home all day I couldn't even bring myself to visit you. Every day that you were in the hospital, I felt a hint of relief that you weren't at home, and then I would feel guilty about how I felt, and it would make it even harder to come to see you. Then once you were out of the hospital, it all changed for the wors... When Kellie called and told me that you are getting out of the hospital and then asked me to come to pick you up, I said no because I couldn't handle seeing you yet. I even wanted to leave the house so when you got home I wouldn't be there. But for some reason I didn't, instead I stayed home, and I cleaned up and got things ready for you to come. I don't know why but I was expecting something to happen when you got home that would change things. But you got home, and nothing changed, well at least it seemed that way to me." She said with tears running down her cheeks.

"What did you want to change, I thought everything was good the way it was, you could have just told me what you wanted, and I would've done my best to change things for you." I replied to her, then reached to wipe her tears away.

"Stop it." She said stopping my hand from reaching her face. I paused as she wiped her face, then turned her back to me. I was quite hesitant for a while, I didn't touch her and I didn't move for quite a while as we sat in silence. Then she stood to her feet and turned to me.

"You got back from the hospital everything changed, you were a different person. But the thing that I wanted you to change remain the same, Kellie was still there, but most of all work was still there. Even though you had taken a break from it, I could see it in your eyes that you still wanted to be at work every day. And every time you said something to me trying to get me to talk to you, I just pushed you away even more. I started to hate you for changing and no longer being my Superman, and turning into someone that was normal." She said to me as the tears started to go away.

She took my hand and pulled me up off the bench, then she hugged me and kiss me on the cheek. As she did, I opened my mouth to speak, but she started to speak before I could say anything. "Honestly, I couldn't take living with you when you were sick I just didn't want to. Every day I saw you, and I just got sadder and sadder, and it made me angry inside, a part of me even started to hate you because you're sick. Will, I just don't know what will happen to us, and honestly I don't know if I can continue this." She said shocking me completely and leaving me speechless.

"I love you, but right now I just need some time to figure things out.

IT WASN'T FATE

I'll call you when I'm ready to talk about things, don't call me." She said to me then turned and walked away, she reached the door and looked back slightly and without any hesitation closed the door behind her quickly. All I could do was watch as the love my life walked away.

Chapter 6

The beginning of a life

The end of a life

For every beginning

There is an end

I start as we end.

IT WASN'T FATE

I sat in my car in complete shock for the longest half hour of my life. My mind ran over everything she had said to me over and over again, killing me with each word that echoed in my mind. I finally managed to lift my hand and start the car, my eyes burled with tears, I pulled out of the driveway.

I pulled onto the road heading towards the high way driving slowly, I didn't know how I would cope with what just happened maybe it was time I gave up on all this I thought as I drove down the road. *"Really, I mean really, I so didn't see that coming. But it's time to get out of this slum you have been in since you had your stroke. Come on now you use to be fun and enjoy your life now all you do is worry and sulk. Now let's start recovering. First thing is first, you're driving a Corvette your dream car, and you're driving it like it's a fifty-year-old tractor-trailer that belongs on a farm. So how about you use those peddles the way they should be."* The voice of Peter said to me out of nowhere.

Then before I could turn my head my foot hit the floor and the car took off. I no longer had a chance to look over to see where Peter was, now all I could do was hold on and dodge the cars that were now flying towards me. In less than a minute I saw the ramp onto the highway, and before I could get to it, I heard police sirens behind me approaching fast.

Before I knew it, I was fully enjoying the ride of my life at over a 150 miles an hour flying between cars, with cop cars trying to keep up behind me. *"See now don't you feel much better, I bet all those thoughts* are gone now?" Said Peter, as a small version of him appeared sitting on the steering wheel. I smiled a bit as I replied. *"What thoughts are you talking about?"*

My mind was clear of all thoughts but the road, and for the first time in a very long time I had forgotten all my problems, at work, with Crystal, everything was gone it was just me and the road. But sadly that would be coming to an end soon as I saw the row of cop cars blocking the road ahead. My little joy ride was over, but at least it lasted a while. I slammed on the breaks and hit the call button on the steering wheel at the same time. The car stopping within inches from the roadblock as Kellie picked up the phone. *"I'm going to need you to come get me out of jail, call you when I get my phone call. Okay, thanks bye."* I said before she could say anything and then hung up in the middle of her yelling what.

Kellie came to bail me out that night, and when I saw her, she was furious. *"What the hell were you thinking you could have gotten yourself killed not to mention you could have killed someone else! I shouldn't have come to get you, maybe a little stay in here would teach you a lesson!"* She screamed so loud everyone could hear her yelling at me. I just looked at her with a sorry look. *"I'm really sorry. But I did spend the time thinking about how things are going in my life, and how they are going in the company, I have an idea that will help me feel better and maybe even get me Crystal back together, and at the same time get this company on the map in a whole new way."* I said looking at her trying my best to get her to stop being mad at me.

Kellie looked at me and just pushed me out. *"Yeah yeah, whatever you say! I don't want to hear it anymore I'll consider listening to you if you have something good to say."* She said as she got in the driver's seat of my car. *"Well get in, you're not driving any more ever again. I'm dropping you home and taking the car with me."* She snapped at me as we drove off.

After a few minutes of driving, she calmed down. *"Well tell me what you were thinking about, you have until we get to your house after that I'm not listening to you."* She said sounding like she was a bit less mad. I did actually have a good idea, or at least I thought it was so I asked my first question before I told her my idea. *"We do have an RND department right? So what do they do?"* I asked her with a confident smile on my face. *"Yes we have one and from what I know of their current work they have been working on building us redesigned servers to allow us to have an interactive publishing site that can build print-ready files for us with half the load as the current one. Or something like that I don't really know all the details, all I really know is they have twenty-five percent of net profit as their budget."* She said answering me sounding a bit confused.

"Perfect, this will work then. I want you to cut their budget to twenty percent and use the five percent that you cut from them for MS research, but I want you to put it in the most radical research you can find. One that is pushing for a cure, and not just a way to slow this thing down." I said to her trying to look as serious as possible. She looked over at me surprised at what I had said to her. *"Well I can work*

on that tomorrow, but you better come into work and get something new done because if you don't, there won't be anything from me to cut from RND." She said as we pulled up and she unlocked the doors. *"Now get out I'm still mad at you. You better be ready early tomorrow I better not have to wait a second for you when I pick you up or I'm making you walk."* She said then speed off.

Chapter 7

The End

This is the end

The end of old

The end of yesterday

The end of today

No more will I look back

No more will I dwell in the past

No more shall I look back

This is the end

The end of who I was

The end of the old me

I am no longer the same

For that me has come to its end.

IT WASN'T FATE

I woke up thinking that the day before was a bad dream I was having. I washed my face and looked out my window, my car was gone, tears started to blur my eyes as the realizations of what had really happened the day before hit me. I headed right back to the bed and flopped down in it with the full intention of not getting back out of it for some time. *"If you don't get out of bed this instant I'm going to make you regret it mister!"* I heard her voice and couldn't believe it, it was Crystal it had to be her. I jumped up with joy and turned to her.

There she was standing in front of the door with her usual look of disappointment she would have when I wanted to sleep all day. I couldn't believe my eyes, and I ran to her to hug her I was so excited.

"AHHH! What just happened my head?" I yelled grabbing my head realizing that I had just run into the wall. I looked around confused to see Crystal sitting on the bed in her underwear smiling. *"Aww, baby did you get hurt."* She said then started to laugh. Now I was confused as to what was going on, why was she acting like this. Her laugh started to change and then she got up and spun around. I couldn't believe my eyes as her body transformed into a guy's body, and her face changed to Peters.

I knew exactly what was going on now. *"Now that you're up why don't you head to work and get some work done. I have a great idea for your next book, I think I want my own space army, and maybe an Armada, something along those lines will do."* He said with a smile on his face that stretched from ear to ear. I just stood there speechless and angry then stormed out the room slamming the door behind me while rubbing my head with the other hand. *"don't forget my big blue ship to."* I heard his voice from behind me.

From that day forward things in my life changed day by day. I no longer spent time laying around sulking or even just having fun to my self-playing games, or watching movies for hours like I used to in my free time. Now my only thoughts were running my company and writing new stories. Every day I spend hours alone writing page after page, then I would spend the rest of the time in meetings. On weekends after I made it home from church, I would be back at it without fail. I had never spent this much time writing before, and before I knew it, I was on my sixth book of the year.

I pulled my draw out as I got dressed and as I did, a picture fell from it. It must have dropped into the draw of the dresser, oh well I'll get it before I leave I thought as I finished getting dressed. I reached for it and stopped as my watch beeped, I had to get going now, or I would be late for the meeting. I grabbed the picture and slid it in my pocket, then headed off to the meeting. It was a very important meeting seeing that was with the head of the company I was giving money to for MS research.

I pulled up to the white building that the company was based out of, it was a long building I had been to before. However, the last time I was, there it looked much different. This was something I paid no thought to however. I was too excited to find out what they had called the meeting for. I walked up to the door, and there were people in lab coats waiting for me. They led me to a small room at the far end of the building and then they just walked away without a word, leaving me standing in front of a blue door that just had the words **Enter When Ready** written across it.

I looked around and didn't see anyone in the hall, so I figured they were in the room. I pulled the doors handle and stepped into the room expecting to see a room full of people, but instead, all I saw was one person sitting in the middle of the room. He spun around in the chair he was sitting in, and for a moment I expected it to be Peter, but thankfully it wasn't. *"Hello, Sir. Will my name is Andrew, I am the head of research in this building. Which thanks to you is no longer a little research facility but the whole building now. But I think the part you will enjoy the most is that we are now the leader in MS research, but the reason we are so excited is because we have just made a major breakthrough."* He said then pointed to the chair that was sitting in the room next to him facing the far wall.

I sat in the chair, and he spun back around, so we were both facing the wall in front of us. The lights flickered and went out then the wall lit up, it was like an old fashion movie it went black and white, numbers flashed on the wall, then the image changed to Andrew. He had a small test tube filled with a blue liquid, then he poured it into a large petri dish. He then starting saying some very technical terms very fast too fast for me to keep up with. All I got from him talking for three minutes was DNA and internal time clock. The screen changed to a zoomed in sample of something. He tapped my shoulder and spoke over the video.

"That's a sample of spinal fluid from a person with stage two MS that has had multiple flare-ups. Now watch what happens." I looked back at the video as what looked like germs dyed blue started to eat the cells in the sample.

I looked over at him confused, and he pushed my head back to look at the video. *"You will want to see what happens next."* What I saw confused me, the blue germs kept expanding around the cells trying to eat them then got to their limit and burst open. Then as they burst, their outer shell stuck to the cells all over the sample. *"What is this nonsense you're showing me, is this a joke or something?"* I said getting a bit annoyed and plenty confused by what I had just seen. He just laughed and got up from the chair and headed to the door. *"Hey, I'm talking to you tell me what's going on here."* I said trying my best not to yell at him, but he just opened the door and walked through it. *"We did it your cured."* His words came sliding from behind the door like a snake hunting its pray leaving me stunned.

I fell back in the chair in shock and disbelief of what was just said to me, then the audio on the video stopped, and the image just stopped. Then one line appeared on the screen over the image. **ALL CELL DAMAGE HAS BEEN SUCCESSFULLY REPAIRED IN CELL SIMPLES TAKEN FROM PATIENTS 01.** Andrew was back on the screen this time with a glass in his hand. *"A toast to the man that will go down in history as the person responsible for curing the world. This will not only rebuild the damaged cells in the brain of MS patients effectively reversing all damage done by the diseases, but it will be able to be used to cure* almost any brain disorder and in a few years anything else we want. Who knows we may even be able to cure death itself, now wouldn't that be something." He said holding up the glass to the camera smiling.

"Now that I can get behind. A cure for death. Well, come on lets toast to them finding a cure to MS and hopefully a cure to death next." Said Peter from the chair next to me holding a glass, I turned not questioning anything and just taking the glass from the small table that was there. "Yeah here's to all that." I said tipping the glass back, feeling something poke at my side as I drank.

I put my hand in my pocket and found the paper that had fallen earlier that morning, I pulled it out and unfolded it. It was the first picture me and Crystal had taken together, I just stared at it, thinking how much of a coincidence it was, maybe this was a sign that we would be getting back together.

A small smile came to my face as I got up from the chair and headed out of the room, maybe after a year and some my life would finally be getting back to normal. I pulled my phone out. **I need to see you.** I wrote in a message and sent it to crystal, and before I could even get to my car it rang, it was a reply from Crystal. **I want to see you too if you're free you can come by now.** My heart froze, and I almost dropped my phone as I read the message. I jumped in the car and off I went to her mother's house.

Chapter 8

From the end we begin

From the beginning we embark

This journey is but a circle

This journey is forever

And each time we reach the end

We embark heading into the circle once more

The circle that always leads to the end.

IT WASN'T FATE

The drive to her house was unusually long almost to the point where I thought I was going the wrong way.

Finally, I pulled up to her house and saw that she was outside just sitting there with something beside her. *"Those look like bags is she planning on coming back just like that after being gone all this time?"* Said Peter from the passenger side. I looked over at him, and a part of me was happy, and a part of me was confused. *"Well what's wrong with that I won't mind if she comes back home with me I will be more than happy if she doesn't."* I said with a hopeful smile. *"I'm going to kill you myself, after what she put you through your just going to go back for more, well fine have it your way."* Peter replied angrily. *"Well, it's not your life its mine your just here because you won't leave me alone."* I said snapping back at him.

He looked right back at me. *"Yeah your right, I'm out of here have a nice life."* He said keeping his eyes on me, then he just shook his head and disappeared. I looked all around the car I even check the glove box and my armrest to see if he was hiding in it, but he was actually gone. But I didn't care he was always getting on my nerves, and my life was getting good again and back to normal.

I took a deep breath and opened the door, fixed my shirt and started to walk to her. The closer I got, the more I became sure that the thing next to her were bags, which could mean only one thing. She was ready to come back home. My heart raced as I thought about it, getting closer and closer to her. I wanted to just run up to her and hug her, kiss her and bring her back home finally.

"Hey." Was the only word that came out of my mouth as I tried to hold back my smile. She looked up at me with a blank expression. "Hey Will, how are you. Come and sit." She said avoiding eye contact, as I sat on the bench next to her. I knew this wasn't a good sign no matter how I looked at it. But I ignored my gut feels, I had hope, maybe she was just worried about asking to come back home with me.

"It's been hard for me lately, there is just so much that I have to do and still thinking about us just makes it take so much longer." She said then paused for a bit, I knew it she wanted to come back home so things can get back to the way they use to be. "It's been hard for me to, I miss you, and all I can do now is work all day and night, every time I stop I just can't take it." I said to her, I was hoping that what I said would trigger something, maybe a hug, or a smile. But her expression didn't change at all.

"I'm moving to Chicago, my plane leaves in an hour."

Her word caught me off guard and stabbed me, my heart stopped, and I chocked on the words I was about to say. I sat there speechless as she handed me a sheet of paper. "Please don't make this harder than it needs to be just sign it and let me catch my flight." She said as I turned over the paper and I read the words at the top. **DEVORSE PORCIDENINGS.** She handed me a pen and looked up at me with cold eyes that I couldn't believe belonged to her. She put the pen in my shaking hands and stood up. "I don't have much time Will I have to get going." She said as a taxicab pulled up in the driveway behind my car.

IT WASN'T FATE

My hand managed to sign the paper, then she pulled it out from under the pen and walked off. The cab pulled away, and I was still sitting with the pen in my hand in complete shock, just waiting to wake up or for Peter to appear and tell me it was him this whole time.

The sun began to set, and I had still not moved from where I was, I didn't even know if I could move any part of my body. No, it didn't matter I didn't want to move ever again it was time for my life to end I had reached my limit. My eyes closed as everything went dark, I felt at peace I knew this was my last moment.

"Wake up you, what is wrong with you. You're lucky I keep track of you or you might have died out there last night." Kellie's voice said bringing me back to reality. *"Wow that was some dream it felt so real."* I said as I tried to sit up, but for some reason, I couldn't. *"Sorry Will, but it wasn't a dream I found you passed out at Crystal's house two nights ago. Our lawyer called me the next day and told me what Crystal did, and I'm guessing that's how you ended up passed out there."* I looked over, and all I could do was cry, no words or sounds just tears running down my cheek.

Kellie took my hand in hers and just sat next to me on the bed. I didn't do anything for the rest of that day, seeing that I couldn't move. Being outside passed out like that had caused a flare up and this time it was very bad, combine that with my depression from what had just happened. I knew I wasn't going to get better I had been living with this hell of a sickness long enough to know when I was in trouble. I was right, the doctors didn't know what to do, and no matter what they tried, I just kept getting worst.

Two weeks passed by and I just kept getting worst, but now I wouldn't let anyone see me not even my family. I was in too much pain, and I wanted death to come and take me more with each passing hour I laid in the hospital bed. I reached my hand over the side of the bed and held onto the wire that was running the breathing machine I was hooked up too. I started to pull as hard as I could, the plug moved slowly, but my weak arms could hardly hold themselves up. Knocking came from the door and then it opened.

"Yep just as I thought." Said a familiar yet unknown voice. A man walked in, at first I didn't know who it was then I remembered him as he started to talk again. *"We haven't had any human test yet we aren't even fully done testing this thing, and you go and do this, I mean I know I told you that we found the cure, but I never said it was ready."* Andrew said to me as he shut the door behind him and locked it. He walked over to my bed and pulled the curtains around and pushed the plug back in all the way. He then wrapped the cord around the side of my bed so pulling it would do nothing. *"What are you doing, leave me alone!"* I said trying to yell but barely getting the words out.

"We have made more advances than we thought possible thanks to the money your company gave us, and we are to close now for you to give up and die, so I'm not letting that happen." He said as he tied my hand that was next to the cord to the bed, then with a smile, he covered my mouth, I felt a sharp pain in my side. I looked over, and the last thing I saw was his smile, then pain and darkness. Maybe it was finally over.

Chapter 9

Storms of life rage on

The rain pours cold as ice

The wind blows everything away

The eye of the storm has passed

Now we await the rainbow at the end.

"What happened to you last night, hey wake up." I heard the voice of a nurse, pulling me out of my sleep. But before I could fully wake up I started chocking, my hand flew to my neck as I gasped for air. The nurse panicked and tried to help me as she yelled for help, doing her best to keep me from hurting myself. The doctors ran into the room confused as to what was going on.

Even after unhooking all the machines from me they were still confused as to how I was able to even breathe on my own, the moving and standing was just unbelievable. Three hours later and they were still questioning me about how it was possible that I was recovered.

Kellie showed up with our lawyer, and I was out of the hospital in five minutes. Andrew was standing outside of the hospital as I walked out, I saw him and walked up to him. *"What did you do to me?"* I whispered in his ear, pretending to stumble forward and grab on to him for balance to hide what I was doing. *"I gave you the cure despite what everyone else wanted to do."* He said to me quietly. I looked back as I saw Kellie rushing over to see if I was ok. *"After all the money I have given you guys, you haven't gotten a cure yet, maybe I should stop funding you!"* I said pretending to be angry as Kellie looked to see if I was hurt. *"You know it's not their fault that you got sick you should be thanking God that you got better in the first place. Instead, you're here blaming the poor guy like he had anything to do with you getting sick."* Kellie said as she gave me an angry look. *"I guess you're right, well I want no more excuse I'm going to double your funding, and you better* have a cure before this year is over." I said to Andrew and walked away looking back with a smile.

The next morning was fantastic, I woke up feeling better than I had years. I had slept all through the night without a single turn or twitch, something I hadn't done since I first got sick. I hopped out of my house and spun around as I walked into my office. *"So what's new today Kellie."* I said as I sat down, looking around at everyone just looking at me. *"Well, the first thing we have to go over is your divorce."* My mood instantly changed and I got why everyone was just staring at me in silence. I didn't know what to say or do, I was still in shock about the whole thing, still thinking it was something Peter did. But now I would have to face it and get it out of the way, which was going to be hard for me. *"I don't know what to do, to be honest, I don't even know what she wants."* I said as I laid back in my chair losing all the energy I just had.

"Let's see according to the papers she filled she just wanted a divorce, but it seems as though her lawyer wanted to get a bit more from you and decided that you should turn over fifty percent of the company to her." One of the people at the table said aloud. Then everyone started talking among themselves. *"We can't let that happen, if that happens we could all be out of jobs, no one knows this company like Will and if he isn't the controlling head of the company, but is instead just part of a split control between him and someone else that left him. It could cause the company to drop in sales from our larger corporate buyers. That and our stocks will take a hit in value"* Said Robert, my lawyer and head adviser to my company.

IT WASN'T FATE

"Well Robert I trust your judgment, do what you think is best, just leave me out of this one I have something I need to finish writing." I said then got up and walked out of the room. My mood was destroyed, and I didn't know what to do anymore, all I could think was just to go home and get away from things. For the next two weeks I stayed home working, I wrote and did all my meeting over the phone or by video calls, I just couldn't bring myself to leave the house. Robert would show up at the end of each day to have me sign the papers and tell me how everything was going, but I didn't listen, I just wanted it to be over.

One month after I got out of the hospital Robert came to me when I was just starting to get back out of the house. *"Well it's nice to see you out jogging Will, I'm glad you're getting out of the house, but I do have some bad news for you."* I stopped jogging and walked towards a bench in the park, and sat down while I unscrewed my bottle cap. *"Well, it's never a good thing to hear that coming for you Robert."* I said then took a drink from my bottle. *"Well out with it, tell me what's the problem."* I said then drank from my bottle some more. *"Okay but I want you to relax ok, the divorce is going to be finalized tomorrow, but here is the bad news. You're going to have to give up the house. I know you don't want to, but I had to give something as not to make things worse, so I gave her the house."* He said to me sounding very proud of himself.

"Well that doesn't sound that great to me if I'm giving her the house, I mean she didn't even want to live in it." I said back to him, there was sadness in my voice from the thought of leaving the house. *"Well I think it's what you need to do to get this part of your life over with and for you to get a fresh start. Tonight will be your last night in that house, and it will be put up for sale in the morning. I want you to go home, take it easy, and get it all out of your system. I'll drop off the keys to your new place in the morning ok."* He said to me then handed me the last paper I would be signing, before everything would be done.

That day I made it home later than usual and just laid in the bed and cried, hour after hour my tears flowed until there was nothing left. In the morning, I would head to a different house, and this home that me and Crystal built together would be nothing but a memory of the past. I laid in the dark, nothing in the whole house was on, and I could hear the smallest drop of a pen. Why is this happening I thought, is this a trick by Peter. As I laid thinking, I remembered what happened with Peter the last time I saw him. He said he wouldn't be coming back and I knew it wasn't a lie.

I was free of my illness and everything else it seemed, I closed my eyes and wondered if it was possible to just forget my whole life. My mind faded away slowly as the darkness in the room put me to sleep.

Act 3

Chapter 1

So short is

The time we have together yet

Excitement is always there.

Prolonging our joys

Has been an easy task

Almost doing itself.

We will

Never stop loving and

I will never give you up for all

Eternity.

IT WASN'T FATE

"Are you ok Will, wake up." My brother said to me, waking me up to a headache like no other. *"What's going on?"* I said dazed and confused. *"You hit your head last night, take this and go take a shower it will help you feel better. Mom said to walk around for a bit after to see if you feel better."* He said to me helping me up and handing me a towel. I walked to the bathroom as I tried to remember what had happened the night before. I could swear I was at my house but wait that's not possible is it I mean last night I was playing a game with my brother and fell or was I doing something else. I stood in the bathroom staring at the sink wondering what was going on I was so confused.

I looked up at the mirror as my head cleared up, and I started to remember the night before. Yes, I was playing a game, that's weird I must have dreamed that stuff about marrying Crystal. Wait did I? I mean it seemed so real, but I can't remember any of it now oh well. *"Hurry up in there we will be late for church."* I heard my mom yelling for me to get out of the shower.

The next day on my way to school, I had almost forgotten everything about Crystal that I had dreamt about and when I talked to her the night before I completely forgot about it. But it wasn't important she was just my best friend, so the dream must have been because I was scared about me and Kellie actually being a couple now. After all, I was talking to Crystal about it the day before in the morning to see if she thought it was a good idea.

"Hey, baby how was your weekend." I said as she walked up to me,

after I had gotten off the bus. *"It was ok, sorry I was so busy but moving here has been a bit hectic I still can't believe that my parents decided to move here, and we ended up going to the same school."* Kellie said as she hugged me and then kissed me. *"Yeah, I know what you mean it was so strange that we would start talking online and your parents just move so close all of a sudden. I still can't believe it sometimes, it seems like fate just wanted us to be together for this to happen."* I said back to her as we walked towards the class buildings.

That day I got home and laid in my bed, my head still hurting but not as much. I played my music as I let my mind wonder about my future, and everything that was happening. To think my last year of high school would turn out like this, the girl I was planning to go visit was now living right next door, not just that but everything else was going great. I was getting a full scholarship to follow my dreams in engineering, and I was the top of my class. This year was going perfect, and soon my whole life would be going perfect too.

Chapter 2

Life is the unexpected journey

From begging to end it is unique

It flows in a straight line

From start to finish

Defining itself as it rides the waves of time

But for some life is circle

Taking a different path each time around.

IT WASN'T FATE

Time seemed to fly by every day, my graduation came and went before I knew it. I started my classes, and before I knew it, I was working at a startup engineering firm. I started saving up for a place of my own as I worked and went to school. At first, it seemed like I would never have enough saved up, so I changed my plans. I decided to just rent a place for now and start doing some work of my own to see if I could get a better start to things for when I finished school. A plan that was going great, as Kellie helped keep me motivated and on track.

After a few months of working on all kinds of different projects while in school, and still working it started to get a bit too much, I had to give up one of them. I sat in my class thinking about what I should do, the best thing I thought was going to be to give up my projects that I was trying to do and just finish school and then get back to them. I got home and sat at my computers and waited, I didn't know what I was waiting for, but I felt as if I should be waiting. I opened my Bible and started to read maybe I would be able to figure out what to do after reading, it always helped me before. After a few minutes of reading my head began to hurt and I laid back in the chair, it had been a long day maybe I'm just tired. I took a deep breath and felt a bit better, then I began to stand to my feet taking a deep breath as I did.

A sudden shock of pain rippled through my body, I grabbed my head and screamed out. I staggered around the room looking for my painkillers, after what felt like an eternity I found it and the bottle was to my mouth before I knew it, I didn't even feel it as I swallowed a bunch of them and dropped the bottle. I managed to make it to the bed to sit before the pain rippled out from my head and through my whole body like a wave. I screamed out as loud as I could then I just felt cold darkness. I was pulled into a cold dark world, where I was being pulled apart over and over again. Was I dead, was I in Hell now, the pain grew and pushed away those thoughts quickly.

Time flowed like a rushing river filling me with a lake of pain and drove me to the edge.

My eyes opened as there was a knock on the door. *"Hey Will are you in there are you ok. I've been calling you all day."* Kellie's voice said as she walked in the room. *"Yeah, I think so I just had the worst dream of my life."* I said sitting up thinking about the hell I just went through, it didn't feel like a dream, but I didn't want to tell her what I just went through. *"Okay well come on we are going to be late for your presentation."* I jumped up and grabbed my computer, I had completely forgotten about my presentation that I was supposed to do at school that morning, I just hoped I wasn't too late to do it.

My presentation finished, and I had an idea about what I was going to do now. Well, it was an idea about how to make up my mind on what to do about everything. I had one last project to do, and after this one, if things didn't go well, I would stop my side projects until I finished all my classes. That night I got home and started to do my work on this new project, at first I had no idea what I would be doing, but I knew it was something big. I ran pipes all around the living room, then I got my saw, cut the tops off, and overlapped them forming a grid. But I still wasn't sure what it was going to be. But I had done enough, and I needed to get some sleep anyway.

I woke up that morning with an idea in my head that I couldn't fully figure out, I just knew I had to build it, and so I did. I covered the grid of pipes with clear hard plastic, and then I sealed it so it would be airtight. Then I flipped it over and put tiny holes in the bottom of the pipe every six inches. After hours of working on it, I finally finished the holes and was utterly lost. I had just made a huge grid with hundreds of pipes that had holes on one side and a clear sealed side.

The next week I spent every bit of my free time working on it, first I ran small tubes to all the holes and sealed them, I added a base then attached the sides with the tubes to it to make it the bottom and then added four larger holes to the clear glass at the four sides. I sat and looked at what I had just made and wondered what it was, as far as I could tell it wasn't anything important or useful for that matter. *"I knew it this thing is useless, great I just wasted all my time on this thing for nothing."* I said to myself sitting on the ground next to it.

I sat there for some time thinking about what it could be then I called Kellie. *"Hey, babe wanna do something I'm stuck on this project."* I said to her as she answered the phone. *"Sure I'll be over in a few minutes I know just what to do."* She said then hung up the phone. I pulled my invention outside and sat it close to the trash so it could be thrown out. *"Well I tried, guess it wasn't meant to be."* I said as I looked up at the dark clouds above my head.

Kellie showed up, and we headed to the beach to watch a boat show. As the boats passed by it began to rain slowly at first then a little bit harder after a few minutes. We stayed and watched the boats pass by in the rain for a while then headed back to my place to watch a movie. *"Isn't that what you made, why is it by the trash?"* She said as we walked up to my door. *"Oh yeah, it is what I made but it's useless, and it doesn't matter now it's all wet anyway."* She didn't say anything back just gave me a disappointed look. I knew she wanted me to make something of it, but I didn't know what to do with it.

A few days passed, it was the day the trash would be picked up. I had forgotten everything about taking out my trash, I ran out of the house to throw away my trash before they came. And I saw it there, it had changed colors since the last time I saw it, the pipes were now all green. Then it hit me I knew what it was. I grabbed it and pulled it back to my place it was quite a bit heavier filled with water than when I made it. I set it in the center of my living room and ran around the house getting my tools. *"Man I can't believe I didn't see it when I made it, I almost lost all this time."* I said as I fixed the problems on it and sealed the four holes at the top with four longer tubes in them, then making it airtight. Then I got a small air pump that was left over from the aquarium I had before moving and attacked it to the bottom where all the little tubes joined together.

I plugged it in and watch the air bubble go through the grid. *"It's not useful, and it's not original, but I did finish something, and it does have a purpose."* I said, as I looked it over then pulled it to my small porch. I spent the next few days getting it up on top of my porch and running the four tube from the top inside. *"What happened I thought it was useless? Why is it on the top of your porch now?"* Kellie said as she looked at it while we ate. *"Well it isn't, I figured out what it was after all. Turns out it's an algae farm."* I said to her as I pointed to the small bit of green that was showing. *"Why would you build that, actually forget that why would you need that Will?"* She asked me. *"I don't know I thought it would be cool to keep it, it does produce oxygen so I figured it couldn't hurt to have it."* She just laughed and shook her head at what I had said.

Chapter 3

Brought together by fate and love

Two souls become one

Sitting aside all but their love

Together they shall overcome anything.

IT WASN'T FATE

Life had started to change for me now, I was getting closer and closer to the end of my classes, and I was moving up in my job too. Life was going great everything that I wanted from my life was starting to come through, and what made it all the more amazing was me and Kellie were closer than ever. We were spending almost every day together, going to random places just to go there and having fun. The weeks and months passed by quickly with ease, as my life grew into what I wanted.

My graduation was now two weeks away, and I was going crazy trying to get ready for it, which all my classmates thought was a crazy thing. I was already at the top of my class, and there wasn't much left of the classes, even if I didn't finish the last few assignments, I was still going to finish at the top of the class. I spent day after day at my desk for the whole two weeks, I finished everything I had left to do then started working on a design. With each day I worked on it became clearer it was like the last one I made, I wouldn't know what it was until I was done.

My graduation day came, and as I got home that day, I felt terrific. I sat at my computer desk, and I decided it was time to do the last thing I wanted to do to make my life perfect. I looked around online and found the perfect one, it would be great, and in one week I would get it.

My package came in the mail a week and a half later annoying me because of how late it was, but I didn't pay it much attention. I opened it, and the doorbell rang then the door started opening, it was Kellie opening the door. I ran to the kitchen and opened the first draw, then pushed the package in it, the door swung open and Kellie saw me pushing it away. *"Trying to hide something from me I see you over there honey."* She said trying to see what I was putting in the draw. *"Hey do you wanna go out to dinner tonight, I haven't celebrated my graduation yet you know."* I said playing it off like she didn't see anything. *"Oh yeah that's true, so where do you want to go honey, maybe we can go see a movie."* She replied smiling hugging me. *"Well, I was thinking we can go to the fair I haven't been there in a while."* I said to her.

Kellie was beyond Excited to go to the fair that night, it was one of her favorite things to do. We got there, and we were having so much fun, getting on rides and eating all kinds of junk food. We lost track of time, and before we knew it, the park was starting to get ready to close. *"Honey lets go on one more ride ok, come on the fairs wheel has no line."* I said pulling her behind me heading towards it. We got there and the guy was packing his stuff up, Kellie saw him packing up and fronded as she tugged on my arm for us to go. I just smiled at her and walked up to the conductor. *"Hey you want to make an extra hundred today, let us on, then stop the ride after a few minutes, then you can pack up, and after your done, you can turn it back on and let us off. Sound good?"* I whispered in his ear, he smiled. *"It's ok I don't need your money no one goes on here anymore, so I was going to leave early. Enjoy just tell me how it goes, so I have something to tell my wife tonight."* He said back to me then opened the rope. *"Two tickets Please."* I handed him the two tickets and the 100-dollar bill I was going to use to bribe him with.

IT WASN'T FATE

We got on the ride, and it went up slowly, I pointed out over the distance at all the lights that light up the ground like the stars in the skies. Then the pod we were in rocked as the ride came to a stop. *"You didn't did you."* Kellie said as she looked down and saw the guy running the ride packing up. *"I don't think he knows the ride stopped honey he's packing his stuff up."* I said back to her as I pointed at him. *"Well, we need to get him to see what's wrong before we get st..."* I cut her words short as I kissed her. *"Honey relax I'm sure he will notice and get the ride back down soon enough, let's not bother him, after all, we did keep him from leaving so we can let him finish packing up before we get his attention. Besides look at where we are what's the rush to leave."* I said as I pulled her back from the side with my arms wrapped around her.

"You know I love you don't you honey." I said to her holding her close whispering in her ear. She turned and kissed me. *"I love you to honey."* She said then laid back and closed her eyes pulling my arms around her. I smiled squeezing her tight. *"I want to be with you forever, you know that don't you?"* I said to her. *"Yes I know, and I want to be with you forever too."* She said back to me kissing my hand. *"So what brings on this romantic side today, I haven't seen you like this in a while is everything ok."* She said looking up at me, I laughed a little before responding to her. *"Yes, honey I am doing great everything is going perfect in my life. There is only one thing that I want now, and everything will be perfect."*

"Oh, really and what is that honey, is it something I can help you get." She replied to me with a smile. *"Well yes, you can help me get it.*

What I want is you." I said then kissed her.

She jumped up. *"Are you saying what I think you are?"* I smiled then the pod we were in jerked pushing her straight into my arms. I caught her and moved close to her ear. *"Yes, honey Will you marry me and stay with me forever."* I said to her with a smile. And all I heard was a cry from her almost screaming. *"Yes, Yes, I will I've been waiting for you to ask me for a while now."* She said crying. I hugged her tight all the way down, we got off, and I smiled at the guy running the ride. *"She said yes, you can tell your wife that."* He just laughed as he spoke. *"Well you two are in for the ride of your lives, may God bless you."*

That night finished amazingly, as we planned the date and Kellie spent the whole night calling all her friends telling them she was getting married. I on the other had just laid back and watched her with a smile on my face I was happy, and nothing was going to ruin my life now no matter what I was going to be happy from this day forward.

Chapter 4

Together at last

No more waiting

No more being alone

For now we are together

We are as one from this moment on

From this moment we travel one path

From the two paths we once traveled

A new path different from both is created

Just for the two of us.

IT WASN'T FATE

Time seemed to finally slow down as we got ready for the wedding, the fast pace of my life for the past few years all but stopped. It was now one continuous moment, I was moving through almost like a never-ending dream. Each day we would make plans, phone calls, and go look at the things we were going to use for the wedding.

I sat in my chair at home the night before the wedding, thoughts flowed through my mind about my life. Was I going to be ok, and did I do everything the right way, I didn't know, but it didn't matter now because I was happy. Ringing came from my pocket, and pulled me from my thoughts. *"Hey Will, are you ready for your big day tomorrow?"* Crystal said when I answered the phone. *"I don't know if I am or not, it's just I knew I was ready when I asked her but now I'm not sure if I am ready to go through with this."* I said to her, all I heard was a laugh then a pause. *"Come on Superman don't tell me you're afraid of something. I thought nothing scared you mister."* She said in reply to me giggling.

I went quite for a while, then I started to speak, but before I could get one word out, she started talking again. *"Your Superman aren't you? Well, maybe I should take your Superman sign away from you seeing that you're not acting like it."* I just laughed a bit. *"Okay I get it, your right there is nothing for me to worry about now. Thanks but I think I'm going to try and get some sleep okay."* I said feeling better. *"Okay, goodnight Superman I'll see you tomorrow and no flying away."* She said laughing then hung up the phone.

The next morning came, and before I knew it, I was standing at the altar waiting for her to walk up. The first stroke of the piano rang through the church, and I saw her white dress flowing from the back of the church as she walked towards me. For a moment everything stopped as hundreds of thoughts ran through my mind. **"My life was going to be completely different now**." I thought as I smiled. *"Are you ready for this?"* Kellie said, taking my hand and turning to me. *"Yes, let's do this."* I replied to her, starting the wedding ceremony. My mind took a trip as I waited to say those two words, everything I had been waiting for was now just two words away.

The instant I said those two words it's like everything changed. All the anticipation and tension I felt for the past few months just vanished from my mind, and was replaced with relief. The after party was even better, everyone was so happy for us it was terrific, and we felt like things were the way they should be for the first time.

We left the after party before it ended, and ran to the car before anyone could stop us. We left in a hurry headed straight for the airport, even though we had booked a red-eye flight we were still running late. But with the help of a few back streets and flooring it on the highway we made it with enough time to check in. Good thing redeye flights don't have many people traveling with luggage's this time of year, or we would have missed the flight.

"We made it in time, but that was so close. I told you we should have left earlier." I said packing the bags in the overhead compartment. *"Yeah maybe we should have, but we are here now, so it's fine. Anyway, I'm going to take the window seat I don't like sitting over in the aisles."*

IT WASN'T FATE

She said while moving around me and sitting down. I sat down and buckled up, I was a bit disappointed I hadn't been on a red-eye flight before, and I wanted to see the view of the city at night, but oh well I'll still be able to see it.

I laid back for a few minutes as the plan finished loading and the flight attendant and captain did their speeches before take off. I felt the plane start to move and turned to the window, but Kellie was sleeping on it. I sighed for a bit, then looked around to see if I could look out any other window, luckily the window in the row across from me was opened, and I could see out of it. I watched as the plane took off and then drifted off to sleep as we moved over open waters.

We would be landing in five hours then we would take a short flight, to the small island we would be staying on for our honeymoon. I wasn't sure what the place was called all I knew was that it wasn't a place but more like a hotel that had an island around it. I wanted to go because it had a beach and it was out of the way, almost in the middle of nowhere.

The plane's wheels hit the ground waking me from my short nap. It was still five in the morning, and everyone seemed like they wanted to go back to sleep me included. Which made the next flight go by in a snap, it was as if the moment I sat down and got comfortable, they were telling me to get off the plane.

I walked out of the airport looked around at the beaches as far as I could see with only one thought in mind. *"I wonder if they have big beds here."* I said, Kellie looked at me with an annoyed look. *"Really is*

IT WASN'T FATE

that the only thing you can think about right now on the first day of our honeymoon." I looked at her with a small smile. *"Sorry hun, I'm just tired from the flight and yesterday. I'll just take a nap, and then we can go to the beach in an hour ok."* I said to her with a smile.

Chapter 5

Seconds to minutes

Our love finds joy in every moment

Hours to days

Our love intertwines as it flows

Weeks to months

Our love grows and blossoms like a rose

Years to a life

Our love will endure.

IT WASN'T FATE

The honeymoon really started the next day when I wasn't sleeping or walking around bumping into things and people at every turn. The first thing I did when I woke up that day was run to the window and pull the blinds. I stared off into the wide-open beach, the crystal clear waters that crashed into the sands below. I hadn't seen anything like this since I left the island where I was born. I smiled daydreaming for a few minutes before the light from outside woke Kellie. *"Honeyy... Why is that open."* She yelled at me throwing one of the pillows from the bed at me. *"Oh come on its time to wake up anyway."* I said to her laughing with the pillow in my hand. *"I don't wanna."* She replied then pulled her head under the pillow.

I got us breakfast and managed to get her out of bed in order to eat. *"So what do you think we should do today, this place is really huge, so there is lots to do."* I said as I ate, she looked up at me and suggested. *"You pick."* It was true that I wanted to pick what to do, but at the same time, I was worried about her not liking what I picked to do. I wasn't that interesting of a person from my point of view, and most of the things I did most people thought were weird. *"It's ok, I'm sure anything you pick I will like, and I doubt there is anything in this place that isn't just amazing so no matter what you pick you can't go wrong."* She said with a smile and got up. *"Now hurry up and pick something I'm going to go shower now."* She continued walking out of the room.

We left the hotel and headed down to the ground floor of the hotel we were staying in, it was a beautiful hotel like no other I had ever stayed in. Nothing was spared when it came to making this place looking beautiful, even the ceiling of the rooms had fancy designs on them. But I didn't come to see the scenery I came because they were doing an early bird show, I knew she would love it. It was her favorite, after all, a musical. It started, and her face lit up as the cast began to sing. She was singing along with the words before I knew it, getting completely lost in the show.

She sang along with the whole show, and when it was finished, she waited to see everyone that was in the show. After that, we went for a walk on the beach, where she sang the songs from the show the whole time as we walked along the edge just out of reach of the water. After an hour, I got tired of the songs and pushed her in the water. *"Ahh, why did you do that."* I smiled and dove in the water right next to her making a big splash. *"Oh no, I'm going to get you back."* She said laughing and chasing me through the water trying to catch me.

That week we spent there seemed to fly by, we were having so much fun, trying to do everything that was on the island to do. We went hiking one day and found a great spot with an amazing view and took hundreds' of pictures. Then played tag, something that even caught me by surprise as to how much fun it is as an adult. Then we came down and sat on the beach below, watching as the dolphins swam around hunting fishes in the shallow waters. We went fishing almost every night after the dolphins left even though we knew we wouldn't catch anything.

We even did the rock climbing wall together, then she watched as

I dove off one of the cliffs that were built into the side of the hotel for base diving. Something I thought was like riding a bike once you do it you can't forget how to do it, well turns out you can forget and Kellie somehow managed to get a picture at the moment I tripped and fell off the ledge. Which was the one picture I tried to get her to delete, but she just wouldn't give it up.

Between the swimming, base diving, tag, daily shows, and so much more we wore ourselves out completely. The week ended and we got back on the plane early in the morning, and before the flight attendees could even finish talking, we were both out cold. Before I could realize what was going on Kellie was pushing me to sit down in the second plane. I was more tired than I had been in years, but that's just because of all of the things I did on the trip.

We got off the plane and headed to the parking lot. *"Are you ok honey, you seem sick staggering all over like your drunk."* Kellie said as I bumped into a car. *"Yeah, I'm ok maybe all the drinks I had this week is hitting me now. But I am exhausted today for some reason but don't worry I'll get some rest when we get home."* I said as I fumbled to get the keys out of my bag. *"Okay give me that I'm driving go sit."* She said to me pointing at the other side of the car then took the keys out of the bag and opened the car. I sat down, and it was as if the chair drugged me because I was asleep as soon as my back touched it.

"Ahhh my head..." I screamed out in pain, jumping up out of my seat and being pulled back down by my seat belt. I heard the cars breaks pull then I felt the seat belt pull me tight pinning me to the seat.

IT WASN'T FATE

Then everything went black for an instant, and then red rushed over me as the pain in my head, shot through my body overwhelming me and pushing me into a world of pain. It got worse with each passing second. I could no longer tell how much time was passing me by, but it felt like years were rolling by me in this world filled with nothing but pain. I couldn't be alive it just wasn't possible.

I couldn't feel my body, all I felt was pain. I must be in hell there was no way I was still alive, time rolled on in this place almost mocking me. Year after year, seem to pass by without end, drifting into each other like one continuous moment of pain.

The pain consumed me completely, and I lost hold of who I was to the pain, drifting through it laughing. *"I remember this HA HA is that the best you got..."* I giggled. *"This isn't my first time in hell you can't scare me..."* **BEEP BEEP BEEP**. The sound pierced through the consuming pain. My eyes opened, and I saw Crystal running towards me, then my version flashed as if I was being pulled back into the hell I was escaping. Then I was in a room with Kellie laying on the bed next to me sleeping. *"What's going on, why don't I know this person next to me?"* My head spun, and I blacked out.

"Wake up Will." Said a voice that I had never heard before, my eyes opened to see a nurse sitting across from me checking my blood pressure. *"Oh I see you're awake now, well that's good I'm glad, your doctor will be in soon, don't try to get up yet."* She said taking the machine from around my arm and got up to check my temperature. Soon after she left the room as Kellie walked in.

Chapter 6

Pain I know all too well

But it is true love that hunts me

Night after night the longing for this

The need for love is killing me

But the pain I suffer keeps me alive

I long for that day when I have true love

Then the pain that destroys this body

Will be nothing but a side note.

"Hey, Will how are you doing today?" Said the doctor walking into the room. I looked up at him trying to sit up with no luck. *"I'm doing ok I feel very weak though, what's wrong with me?"* I said back to him in a weak voice. *"Well I have good news for you, and then I have bad news for you. Which do you want to hear first?"* He asked me closing my chats, then hanging them back on the bottom of my bed. *"Let me hear the good news first."* I said feeling as if my lungs were trying to close themselves as I spoke.

"Well, the good news is that you will be able to leave the hospital next week." He paused for a moment, then continued. *"The bad news is that you have MS, this is your first flare up. Unfortunately, from the damage that has already been done to your brain, it seems like it has been getting worst for almost a year now. Tell me have you been experiencing headaches or problems moving or any problems with your body over the past few months?"* He asked as he moved around getting comfortable in the chair he was in. *"Well no I have been a bit more tired than normal, the past two or three weeks nothing big. But I have been getting ready for a wedding so that can't be related."* I said to him, almost winding myself in the process.

"Well that is interesting, well I do have another question for you, do you know you have a higher oxygen content in your blood than the average person." He said to me, giving me a look of suspicions. I tried to answer him but I didn't have the strength left to say anything else for a while, so I just nodded my head. *"Well, I didn't expect you to know or*

admit it so easily, from my experience having a level this high means the person goes to oxygen bars, which isn't a bad thing but that's usually what they are doing to hide drug problems." He said with a smile. *"So tell me why is yours higher than normal?"* He asked then waited for me to answer him with a very odd smile, it was almost creepy.

"I have a makeshift CO2 scrubber in my house, the oxygen level in the room I sleep in can get up to ten present higher than the air outside." I replied then gasped for air, as I started to get light headed. He got up and left the room without a word, I tried to move my head to see where he went, but I was too weak to move. Maybe what I was doing was a bad idea, I guess I will have to get it taken down when I get home first thing then. I closed my eyes trying to relax and breath, taking slow deep breathes to calm myself, after about a minute it started to get easier to breathe. I began to feel my lungs open up and I opened my eyes to see the doctor in front of me with an oxygen tank.

"Relax, now this should help. After what you told me I realized that you're used to a higher oxygen level in the air than the average person. Which given your current state would make it very hard to breathe without that level of oxygen present." He said then he headed back to the chair and sat down. *"So does that mean I did this to myself?"* I asked finally able to catch my breath. *"Well no actually. Well, that's a tricky question. It is true that higher levels of oxygen can have a beneficial effect on the body and too much oxygen can damage the body. But I wouldn't say that the oxygen did this to you, but at the same time it helped in its own way."* He said which just confused me even more.

114

IT WASN'T FATE

"Well, what I mean is you having MS isn't caused by the oxygen, but the reason you didn't know till now is, because of your unusual home. Your symptoms were masked by the good effects of the oxygen, and combined with the fact that you're in great shape and you don't seem to eat unhealthy based on the results from your blood work. All these things helped you stay just ahead of this illness, but once you went on vacation, it changed. Away from your house and having a lot of junk food weakened you, just enough for it to take a hold and do some serious damage." What he said was a bit hard to understand, but it made sense somehow. I had started feeling tired on the plane which was the first night I had stayed away from my place since I moved in. And the whole week of the honeymoon I felt tired, but I just figured it was because I was having a lot of junk food, and not getting enough sleep.

"So what should I do when I get home, should I change anything so I can get better?" I asked. *"Well you're going to have to take it easy for a while and do your best not to get stressed out over things, also you will have to take a shot every other day to help regulate your immune system. It's not a cure, and it's not a guarantee that you will get better, but it is your best bet to getting better. I'm sorry there isn't much I can do to help you, but we just don't know much about MS so there isn't much that you can do that we know will work for sure, it mostly depends on the person."* He said back to me and waited to see if I had another question, but after a few minutes of silence, I didn't have anything to say.

"The nurse will be in to check on you soon so if you have any more question just ask her and she will pass it along to me, and I'll do my best to answer your questions when I can." He said before getting up and leaving.

I laid in the bed listening to the sound of the machines in my room. The slow hiss of the oxygen tank was almost hypnotic pulling me from my room and off into a daydream about my life. "Hey there are you awake, you look awake your eyes are open." A familiar voice said bringing me out of my daydream. "Yeah who are you and what are you doing in my room?" I said, realizing I had never seen the person before. "Oh come on that hurts my feelings it's me your pal Peter, don't tell me you don't remember me." He said to me with the most unusual smile I had ever seen, it was almost cartoon-like. "No I don't know you I think you're the one that has a problem, I would remember you if I meet you before, now can you please leave my room so I can get some rest." I said to him getting a bit annoyed.

"AWW well maybe next time you will remember me." He said then headed to the door. "And maybe next time I won't have to be gone so long. Okay well, see you later Will." He said then walked out of the room seeming to vanish before he turned the corner. Confusing me for a second but then I realized that the door was closed, it must have been the light reflected from the door why I didn't see him turn and leave.

Chapter 7

The greatest challenge in the universe

Is also the greatest gift in the universe

It is needed by all from birth to death

It cannot be taken or bought

Neither can it be stolen or hidden

It is never hoarded

And it is always freely given

This one thing so great

Yet possessed by the smallest

Is envied even by time

Because it is never hated

Even by those who know only hate

For these reasons, Love is the greatest power in the universe.

IT WASN'T FATE

I left the hospital a week after seeing my doctor. I didn't speak much the last week in the hospital, I spent so much of it resting or sleeping that I don't remember much of what I did. I was ready to get back to my normal life. But I didn't know what I was going to do any different, as Kellie drove us home I thought about what I needed to change and couldn't come up with anything.

"Are you ok over there?" Kellie said as she drove, I looked over to her with a half smile. *"Yes, I'm doing ok it's just that I don't know what to do right now. After all the doctors didn't give me any help, but the nice nurse gave me a card to some company that's doing radical research."* I answered her halfway gone in my mind.

That day we got home, and things were different, I didn't stay up to watch anything with her I just went straight to bed. I slept better than I thought I would that night, it seemed as though as soon as I hit the bed, I was out fast asleep. I woke up dazed and confused, I had a strange dream, where Peter was talking to me about something. *"Man that was a strange dream, I don't even know where any of that came from."* I said as I realized that I was alone in bed catching me completely by surprise. This was the first time I have known her to be up before me for as long as I knew her.

Oh well, maybe she had something to do, I thought. Then turned over in bed and looked at the clock. It read **12:30 PM,** well it could also be because of how late it was. I got out of bed and headed into the kitchen to find a note. **I made you something to eat it's in the**

microwave, didn't want to wake you. I'll see you after work. I read the note as I headed over to the microwave and turned it on.

After eating, I felt a bit more like myself, I still felt weak, but my mind was moving like normal again. I sat down at my desk and turned on my favorite playlist. The songs blasted out from the speakers behind the desk, sending sound wave vibrating through my body. After a few minutes, I got lost in it like I would always do when working on something. *"Man you are jamming, I like your taste in music now. I never use to, but I think I can get use to this."* A voice said from behind me over the music.

I jumped up shocked by the voice, I didn't hear the door open or closed so who was in my house, and it certainly didn't sound like anyone in my family. I spun around in my chair ready to do something, even though I didn't know what I was going to do in the state I was in. *"Who... Wait I know you, how did you get in here."* I said trying to sound intimidating to my best ability. He smiled and twirled around. *"Well I walked in, how else do you get into a house."* He said with a laugh flopping down onto the couch behind him.

"You you your umm Peter the crazy guy from the hospital that thought I knew you. How did you get into my house, are you stocking me now?" I said in my best aggressive tone looking around to see if anything looked like it was broken into. *"Ha ha very funny, do you really think your worth stocking, you act like this is the first time you've seen me. Wait is this your first time seeing me?"* He said sitting forward on the couch. *"I don't know you, I keep telling you that I don't know you,*

but you won't listen to me. The first time I ever saw you in my life was last week at the hospital when you barged into my room." His face lit up, and he was off the chair in an instant in front of me with his hand out.

"I'm Peter, it's nice to meet you Will even though I know everything about you already. Come on now don't leave me hanging." He said with that creepy smile that his face seemed to wrap around. I reached up and shook his hand. "Yeah hey Peter, now why are you in my place, and how did you get in?" I said to him as he just shook my hand looking straight at me smiling with his mouth open. I looked at him, then yanked my hand away hitting it on the desk behind me. "Be careful man, don't want to break your computer just when you were going to make something." He said then walked back to the couch and flopped back down on it. "So what are you making anyway?" He said looking around at everything in the room.

"What I'm making doesn't concern you. And you didn't answer my question how did you get in here?" I said to him getting a little more than annoyed. He just looked over at me and laughed laying back in the couch and putting his legs up. "That does it. I'm calling the cops!" I yelled grabbing my phone from next to the computer. "Oh really now, and what are they going to do. You know you use to be more fun." He said then got up and walked up to me. "I get it I'll leave, see you next time." He said inches away from my face then smiled his huge smile and walked out to my porch. Opened the door and then jumped off. I got up and ran to the door almost running right into it. "How did he do that the door is still locked." I pulled the door open, looked over the side, and saw nothing.

I looked around for a few minutes to see if I could find where he had run off to, then headed back inside and checked all my doors and windows. I sat back at my desk I had forgotten what I was going to work on. So I just looked at the screen and waited. After an hour, I started my music back but not as loud this time, if he came back, I wanted to know where he was coming in from so I can catch him and call the cops.

I stared at the picture of a Corvette on my desktop thinking about what I wanted to design. *"Ahh! Something come to mind please, come on please I can't just sit at home like this it's going to drive me crazy. Ahh! I'm already talking to myself."* I said as I ran my hands through my hair. *"Well, I'll make a car and get rich."* I said laughing then leaning forward in the chair. It wasn't a bad idea, I mean I could do it seeing that I had no other ideas.

Kellie got home soon after I started work on my car, and I stopped to eat and tell her about what had happened that day. At first, she thought it was a joke then when she realized I was serious she went running around the house looking to see where Peter might have gotten in. *"That's it tomorrow I'm staying home with you and calling the hospital, I'm going to see who this Peter is."* She said looking all around, not once looking at me.

Chapter 8

Time never ceases

Forever untamed

In this endless universe

Accompanied by none

While all strive to control it

It sits atop its pedestal

Looking down with eyes of envy

Upon those with love

For it knows it's the one thing

That it's mighty hands cannot turn to dust.

IT WASN'T FATE

I woke up the next morning once again alone in the bed, this time however there was a note on the bed when I woke up. **I'm in the living room whenever you wake up.** I read it then headed to the bathroom to wash up, and then I sat on the bed for a minute. *"You know it don't you, something is wrong. It's just what you were thinking wasn't it."* I heard the voice as I was stretching touching my toes. I knew who it was and yelled out, jumping up and falling back on the bed. *"I'm going to call the cops, I'm going to make sure you don't come back here again."* I said to Peter looking for the phone, Kellie burst into the room, and as she saw me on the bed, she had a horrified look on her. *"Don't just stand there honey call the cops!"* I said in a frantic panic.

She looked at me on the bed confused. *"Are you ok honey?"* She said in a scared voice. *"Now's not the time honey, I'm fine, can't you see he's back, call the cops already."* I said to her looking over at him. He was just laughing. *"Why are you laughing, you're going to jail!"* I yelled out to him, then turned to Kellie who was now walking to me slowly like there was something wrong with me. *"What are you doing, what's gotten into you?"* I asked her, as she got closer and took my hand. *"It's ok I'm here, relax it's ok now."* She said as she pulled me close and hugged me.

"Oh man you are funny, forget what I said yesterday I think I like you better now. I can't believe you don't get it." He said falling to the floor laughing. *"What's going on?"* I said, she let me go and leaned back. *"There is no one here, it's just you and me honey."* She said with

a scared look on her face. Peter got up off the ground and jumped onto the bed right next to me and tapped her on the head then smiled. *"She can't see me Will I love this I mean come on didn't me walking in yesterday give it away, or the fact that I walked through a locked door. I mean come on it was kind of hard to miss with the clues I gave you."* He said as his creepy smile rolled from one ear to the next.

"No this can't be, he's right there on the bed. No, I won't accept this why are you doing this to me." I said pulling away from Kellie and moved to the corner of the bed. *"Its ok Will come we can go to the hospital and see your doctor."* She said to me trying not to move towards me too fast. I just pulled my feet up and stayed still. She gave up on getting me to come to her after a few minutes and left the room. Then she came back in the room dressed and put my shirt over my shoulders. *"Come we have to go now."* She said in a calm, low voice. I was lost looking at Peter just sitting on the side of the bed smiling, I held on to her and moved away from him slowly and out of the room.

The visit to the doctor went very bad, to say the least. After that morning I didn't think there was anything anyone could do to get me to feel better. But Kellie tried the whole day, but it wouldn't work, and whenever it seemed as if I was starting to feel better Peter would try to say something to me and I would pull away again. I wouldn't say anything to anyone, not even Kellie, I just didn't know what was real anymore.

This went on for two weeks before I started to get used to seeing Peter, and finally, I spoke again. *"Good morning."* I said as I walked out of the room that morning, Kellie was sitting at the table. *"Good morning how are you feeling do you want something to eat?"* She asked as she got up from the table. *"No sit back down its ok I think I am ok now, did you eat yet?"* I said as I walked to the kitchen. *"No, not yet I just woke up a little while ago."* I looked over at her as I walked in the kitchen. *"Good well sit I'll make you something."* I said then took a pan out to start cooking.

I opened the fridge, and when I closed it, Peter was standing right behind the door. I saw him and jumped a little but didn't say anything. I looked over his shoulder to see if Kellie saw me jump. I didn't think she did so I turned and ignored him. *"Aww come on man, you can't keep not talking to me I mean I am part of you. Well I know you won't talk with her here so just let me talk, I think you need to get back to work, I mean that car you had started was a great idea. I think you need to get it finished."* He said to me then walked out of the kitchen.

After that day, I didn't see him like I did every morning when I woke up. And I got back to myself well mostly back to myself. Enough for Kellie to go back to work, and for me to try to get back to doing something. I sat at my computer and then got on my phone and called up the company I worked for and asked them to send me something to work on. Then I just laid back in my chair with my eyes closed blasting my music to drown out all my problems, trying to forget the past few weeks. **Beep.** *"I think they sent you something."* I heard Peters voice from behind me. I leaned forward and looked at my computer. My boss had sent me some drawings that he wanted to me to come up with a 3D build ready design for.

"*Well, Peter what do I have to do to get rid of you?*" I said as I started up my programs to start working. "*Nothing, I like it here I don't think I'm going anywhere.*" He said with a smile. "*Great that's nice, well will you at least be quite so I can get my work done?*" I said back to him. "*Sure why not, I have some work to do to. All I wanted was for you to relax and accept that I'm here.*" He said back to me appearing in front of me smiling, then vanishing. I turned, and he was there on the couch with a computer in his lap. I opened my mouth to speak then just stopped.

Kellie got home that day, I felt different like I was ready to be me finally, she walked up to me. "*Sorry Will I'm tired I just want to lay down for a while.*" She said to me and went straight to the room. So I made her something to eat and took it to her, maybe she will feel better after she ate. But it didn't work she just laid in bed like something was wrong but no matter what I asked she didn't say anything.

A few weeks passed, and everything got better again we were talking and doing some of the things we use to do. But I felt like something was still wrong as if she was holding something back from me. But no matter how many times I asked if there was something wrong she would just brush it off and tell me everything was great. Our first Thanksgiving came, and she was off. "*Honey I'm going to see my grandma after this ok. I haven't seen her in a while, and I want to.*" I smiled. "*Sure, is that why you have been acting weird lately because you wanted to go see your grandma onThanksgiving.*" She just looked at me a bit relieved then smiled.

After that things changed, everyday things were starting to get so much better. I was working from home and designing my car with Peter's help, well it was mostly his idea, but I was doing the work, which seemed weird seeing that he was in my head.

The time passed by quickly and soon The New Year was coming up faster than I could get ready for. As it approached faster and faster I couldn't help but feel that I wanted to do something new and important , so I called up the number on the card I had gotten from the nurse. *"Hey, I got this card from a nurse, and I was wondering if there was something I could be a part of."* There was silence on the line, and I thought that it went dead, then a voice started to speak. *"Umm, well we need a few test subjects for our new drug. Come by the address on the card when you can to sign up."* The voice said then the line went dead. A bizarre thing for a company of any kind to do I thought but didn't pay it any attention.

The next morning I headed down to the address on the card. It was a large white building with blue strips running from the bottom to the top every few feet. I walked up to the door, and as I was going to enter, Peter appeared. *"Are you sure about this, I have a feeling once you enter this place you're not going to be the same person after."* He said blocking the doorway, I paused for a moment. *"I think it's time things were a little different, anyway I got used to you so there isn't anything I can't get used to at this point."* I said to him then pushed the door open and walked in right through him.

IT WASN'T FATE

There was only a lady sitting at the desk, she pointed to the end of the hall, I walked down the hall and came to a door with a sign on it with three words written on it in blue letters. **ENTER WHEN READY**

Act 4

Chapter 1

Love is found at last

Never to be lost again

To be protected forever

For it is precious

Without it this universe has no meaning.

IT WASN'T FATE

The year came to an end before I knew it. I was working hard on finishing up my car design, getting more detailed with each day. While going into the strange office to get blood drawn for the research every few days. Then I had to work on the projects that I had for my actual job, all while finding new things for me and Kellie to do.

I decided to send out my car design to the large car companies, maybe one of them will see it and decide to hire me. Well that was what I was hoping for anyway. After the year started I gave up on that little dream and focused on my actual job and getting healthier. *"Hey, cheer up they will call soon, but more importantly, has that company made any progress on getting you better. I mean they keep taking blood but never give you anything to take."* Peter said to me, actually looking serious something I wasn't used to. *"Yeah, I guess they are they said they will give me something next month, maybe I will be able to feel better for my birthday."* I said with a hopeful smile, as I read over my emails to see what I had to do that day.

I finished reading and started to work on something new, it was like the first time when I made the CO2 scrubber. I had no clue what it was or how it would function. I didn't have anything else to do that day, so I just kept on working on it and by the time Kellie got home I was fifty-five parts in. *"Hey Will we have to talk."* She said as she walked into the room. *"Okay, let's talk. Is there something wrong?"* She looked at me paused for a minute then just said. *"Oh no I just wanted to tell you I was going to see my dad for a few days."* I could see in her eyes that there was something wrong that she wasn't telling me, but I didn't ask I figured there was something wrong with her dad. That afternoon she packed some clothes for the morning.

I woke up the next morning to an empty bed, I looked around, and there was a note on the bed. **Sorry I have to run, I need to get there before 12.** *"I guess she didn't want to tell you the real reason she left early."* Peter said appearing at the bottom of my bed. I looked at him and didn't say anything at first. *"How about we just get some work done, or you could go do whatever it is you do when you're not here."* I said to him and got out of bed.

That day was going pretty good, I still didn't have any work to do so I was just working on my new design. **BEEP BEEP.** My cell phone went off but I was caught up in my design, and I didn't stop for a while to see who it was. I saw that it was Kellie saying hey. I replied saying sorry for taking so long to reply. Then I got a message back. **It's fine I have something to tell you.** I looked at the phone. *"She probably misses me so don't even give me that look."* I said to Peter. **Yes honey what do you have to tell me?** I replied spinning around in my chair to Peter who was holding a model of something in his hand that I had just designed. *"What is this thing anyway?"* He said as the phone went off again. *"I don't know Peter now come on if I knew what it was I'm sure you would know to."* I said picking up my phone.

I can't do this anymore, it's too much for me to deal with. The message hit me hard, and I replied as fast as I could. **What are you talking about deal with what?** As soon as the message went through,

I got another message. **I can't keep lying to you and I can't deal with you.** I was shocked and was speechless for a moment. **Honey what can't you deal with and what are you lying about.** I was starting to shack wondering what was going on, then the next reply came in. **It's over, I don't want to be with you anymore.** My heart stopped, and I dropped my phone, I didn't know what to say for a moment, but I managed to reply somehow. **Whatever it is I'm sure we can work it out.** I sent back then about a minute later I got a message back. **No we can't just stop I can't do it anymore!** I was stuck. **No don't do this to me please.** I replied, I got nothing back for two long minutes.

I cheated on you on Thanksgiving now leave me alone. Her reply came like a knife cutting me in half leaving me shaking. My phone fell to the ground, and I couldn't move. I fell back, luckily into my chair. I just sat there for hours, as Peter tried to get me to get up.

My phone rang, and I expected it to be Kellie telling me it was all a prank. But it wasn't it was a number I didn't know. I picked it up and looked at it for a moment. *"Answer the phone!"* Peter yelled, I pushed the button and put it to my head. *"Hello"* came out of my mouth without me even realizing it. *"Oh hello is this Mr. William?"* The voice shocked me by what she said. *"Yeah, that's me why."* I said back. *"Oh good, I'm calling on behalf of GM in regards to the design you sent us."* My mouth stopped moving, I was lost for words. *"Yes did you review my design?"* The words came out of my mouth without my control.

"Yes we would like you to come down to our local office and talk to one of our design technicians, we are quite interested in your design."

IT WASN'T FATE

She said then it went silent, I was in a shock for a moment, well a little more than a moment. *"I will take that as a yes, it's ok you don't have to say anything just come down and let the technicians talk to you ok Mr. William or do you like Will better."* I was still lost for words. *"I like Will better."* I managed to say almost stuttering. I hung up the phone a few minutes later after getting all the directions. I looked up at Peter, he had a smile that was touching his ears straight out of a cartoon.

Chapter 2

Love and pain

They intertwine into one

Pushing and pulling at each other

One will overcome the other

Warping and twisting

Chocking the life from the other

The one that is stronger will remain

The one that is feed will be stronger

So which one will be feed.

IT WASN'T FATE

The next morning I woke up and headed right to the GM office that the lady told me to go to. I didn't stop to think about anything I just couldn't, I needed to have a clear mind. Which meant no thoughts about Kellie, and no thoughts about my life until the meeting was over.

I pulled up to the building and looked at the big GM sign, then took a deep breath. *"You better not mess this up ok, because if you do I am not putting up with you complaining about this for the rest of your life, you got that."* Said Peter, sitting in the seat next to me with the most serious face I had ever seen him have. Though it wasn't completely serious, it wasn't a goofy face like the one I was use to him having. *"Shut up Peter, I can handle myself ok."* I said back to him a bit annoyed and worried about what was going to happen. *"Yeah, you got this like you had the phone call yesterday right. Just don't do anything dumb. Oh and I'll leave you alone, so you have no one to blame but yourself if this goes wrong."* He replied then vanished from the car.

I walked up to the door of the building and pushed the door open slowly. The door swung slowly as I pushed it, my heart beating faster the wider the door opened. Once it was fully opened, I thought my heart was going to burst out of my chest right into my hand, then wave a little white flag and give up. But it didn't, and I took the first step into the building.

I looked around, and I saw a woman at the front desk, I walked up to her. *"Umm I'm William, I was told to come here today."* I said in a low voice doing my best to hide how nervous I was. She looked up at me with a smile that brightened the room. *"Yes, we have been expecting you Will right this way."* She said as she got up and headed down the hall. At the end of it was a door with nothing written on it, I took a glance around, I saw that it was the only door with nothing written on it. I looked over to her to see if this was the right door. *"Yes this is the right one just go in, someone will be with you in just a few minutes."* She said then pushing the door open a little.

I stepped into the room and looked around, in the center of the room was a large box of some kind, or maybe it was a very tall table, then closer to the door was two chairs. I walked up to one of the chairs and sat down. *"Oh this is a nice office, but everything being white is kind of creepy like some kind of CIA clean room where they take you to extract information in excruciating ways."* Peter's voice came from the chair next to me, I turned slowly pretending to just be looking around the room in case they were cameras in the room. *"Oh relax, they aren't any cameras in here. Hum Well I don't think they are but, its ok don't talk to me, this place is nice."* He said as I just stared right at him trying to burn a hole in him with my eyes. *"Ok ok, I get it you want me to go. You know I might be in your head, but you can't burn holes in me you don't have superpowers your just weird."* He said then got up and walked to the box in the middle of the room and vanished.

The door opened a few minutes later, I turned and in walked two people a tall man who must have been seven feet tall followed by a short woman not even five feet tall. Something I didn't expect to see, they walked up to me and didn't introduce themselves instead they started talking about my design. One question after another they went on none stop. From how was I balancing the weight of the car to what I was expecting to use as the power supply system.

After more than an hour of talking about my design, they stopped asking me questions and just stayed quite for a while. I didn't know if they wanted me to say something back or if I was just supposed to be quiet. After a minute or so, the woman started to speak. *"Well, it looks like they are no more questions for you, well none we can ask you without first asking you this one. Would you like to sell your design to us?"* She said and waited for me to reply to her. *"I I I... I would love to."* I managed to say while stuttering over my words.

The smile on my face at that point was unbelievable. I was grinning as wide as ever. *"Well is there anything that you have to ask us."* The man said as he closed his book. *"Well I would like to name the car is that ok?"* I said hoping and wishing I was going to hear a yes. *"Well, it's not like you can call it anything but you can give us some names and our marketing department will pick the best name from the ones you give us."* He replied. *"Yes!"* I yelled out catching the two of them by surprise. They laughed as I jumped up and down with joy.

After I finished my little celebration, they had a few more questions for me that I answered, then a contract for me to sign, and a few more legal documents that needed to be signed before work on the car could even begin to be thought about.

I got home that afternoon and sat at my desk, I looked down at my phone and what happened yesterday came to mind, then I just started to work on the project that I had no clue about. All I knew was I had to finish it, and I wanted it finished as fast as possible. The more I worked on it the less I thought about Kellie making me keep going with even more focus. Soon I lost track of time, and before I knew it, it was already three AM. I saved my work and headed off to bed, the next day was going to be a big day, and I wanted to get some rest before it started.

Chapter 3

From time to time

There is love

There is pain

There is longing

There is joy

There is togetherness

As time passes from time to time

Everything changes

But it will always remain the same.

IT WASN'T FATE

I woke up late jumping out of bed, and running to my computer. *"Clam down man do you really think you need to be in a hurry after all you did, you already did most of the designing work for the car already. Besides they need to go over the 600 parts of the design before they can even start working on anything."* Said Peter, sitting on the side of the computer desk.

"I guess so, but I should check still." I said opening up my computer and logging into my email. My email loaded slower than usual, and I expected hundreds of emails to pop up, but only two showed up. The first email was from the GM so I, of course, opened that one first and read it as I brushed my teeth. It wasn't anything big it was just a copy of everything I had signed the day before and a pay stub that red twenty-three million postmarked for two weeks from now.

I saw the numbers with all the zeroes behind it and fell back on the floor, I didn't think that they were going to pay me this much. I managed to get back up and finish getting ready for my day. I knew I still had one email left, but I didn't want to open it, I was just too scared to face the fact of Kellie and me right now. I ate and stared at the title of the email the whole time wondering what could be written inside of it, and I couldn't think of anything else. Then Finally, I decided to open it up and take a look at it. **"Will I'm sorry but I will do whatever it takes to make it up to you and win your trust back."**

"Don't fall for it man you know this will only end badly just get out while your still ahead, just cut your losses Ok? Look at what's going on

in your life now, just move forward it will be hard, but you have to."
Peter said to me from behind my shoulder. I turned to him and was
going to tell him to shut up, but I knew what he was saying was what
I was thinking deep down. *"It might work ok I want to try and make
things work out."* I hit the reply button and sent a message. **"It will be
hard and I don't think I can trust you again but I am willing to try and
make things work."** Then I hit send, and it was done.

I went back to working on my design after sending the email. I
didn't know what it was still, but I knew I was almost done with it. I kept
working all into that night while checking to see if Kellie had sent a reply
to my email. I worked and worked until I could hardly see the screen any
more from how tired I was.

"Hey wake up Will, it's time we get some work done." Peter said,
waking me out of my dreams and confusing me on how he was able
to wake me. *"What are you talking about get work done? I don't have
anything to do."* I said to him as I waved my hand through his body as if
he was an alarm clock I was trying to snooze.

DING DONG the doorbell went of waking me back up just as I
started to fall back to sleep. *"Ahh! who could that be and why so early in
the morning, can't I just get some rest without anyone bothering me."* I
said as I reluctantly got out of my bed and headed to the door. I flipped
the lock and opened the door, in front of me was Kellie. I didn't expect
her to come back already, but I wasn't going to say anything, after all, I
did want things to work.

We didn't talk for a while, we just sat there in silence waiting for the other person to start the conversation. After almost an hour, I decided that I would be the one to start things off. *"Well I'm going down to the office of the people doing all that MS research this afternoon, would you like to come along with me."* I said to her, not really hoping for a yes or no, just really anything to break the silence. She looked up at me from staring at the candle on the table. *"Yeah sure I'll come, did they find anything that can help you yet, or are you still just going by giving them blood to run more test."* She said back to me, which started a conversation about how many times I had been there just to give blood and have them run MRI's and cat scans on me.

It wasn't too long after that we headed down to the office. I walked in first to see if the normal person I would always go to was there, or if I would have to wait. But he wasn't, and I had to wait for the head doctor. After about a half an hour, he walked up to me. *"Hey my name is Andrew, I am the head of research here. I heard your Will. You're the one guy that keeps coming back to let us run any test we want on you."* He said and gesturing his hand for us to follow him as he turned. *"Well thanks to you oddly enough we were able to test a lot of different things, it's funny your blood samples last longer than everyone else's does for some reason, I'm guessing that extra oxygen in your home has something to do with that but it's not what we want to talk to you about."* He said as he opened a door with nothing written on it and walked in.

It was an odd room for a research facility, there wasn't much in the room, but it didn't look like a clean room it looked like a break room you would find at an average workplace. *"So what do you have in store for me today?"* I said as I looked around the room at all the pictures of buildings on the walls, something I thought was out of place. I would have expected pictures of cells or brains or something of the sort. *"Up until now, we have been testing on cells and then testing on different animals to see the side effects of the drugs that showed promise. But seeing that MS is not something we can give to an animal the only way for us to test anything for sure would be to test it on a Human. We would like that human to be you."* He said sitting in one of the chairs and getting comfortable.

I was a bit shocked, and I didn't quite know how to reply. *"So what are the risks and side effects of this drug?"* The words came out of my mouth without me even knowing what was going on. Andrew started to tell me about the drug, but I didn't pay him much attention, I was too busy trying to figure out why I said that. Then Peter appeared standing next to Andrew. *"Don't blame me, something had to be said, and I think you should do it. Maybe this is what you need to change your life and get it perfect ish, who knows you might even get the girl."* He said raising his eyebrows and smiling his normal ear to ear smile.

"Okay I think I will do it, when do you think this drug will be ready for me to start." I said to him trying to smile, but it was just a nervous look, as if I was going to jump off a cliff for the first time. *"It will be ready for you in the morning it's kind of a tricky medicine, so it has to be administered in a special way. So if you want to go ahead with it come tomorrow morning with a change of clothes."* He said to me being as

vague as possible as to what was going to actually happen.

Soon after I was on my way home, Kellie didn't say anything the whole ride, but I was too lost thinking about the next day to even realize that she didn't. We got home, and things were actually going better than I thought she cooked while I worked on my design that I still didn't know what it would be, but I knew I only had a few pieces left before it would be done.

After eating, I went back to work and spent hours working forgetting about the next day. I worked without stopping until I finished the last part at 2:35 AM I saved my last file and looked at the folder with all the parts, seven hundred and thirty-five pieces in the folder to build one thing. I shut down my computer, and I crawled into bed, almost forgetting that Kellie was in it again.

My alarm woke me the next morning and Kellie was already up and was making breakfast for us. *"Hurry up and get ready we have to leave soon it's already ten you know."* She said as she put the plate on the table and sat down to eat. I rushed to get ready and eat as fast as I could then we headed out.

I showed up to the building not knowing what to expect at all, but I figured it must just be a few shots and then I would leave. I walked in the door, and I knew it wasn't going to be that simple when the first thing I saw was the two people that I saw often dressed in hazmat suits. *"Umm should I be worried is everything ok?"* I asked the guy in the suite in front of me. He jumped back a little and laughed. *"Oh, it's just you. There is nothing to worry about this is actually to keep us from touching you before we get started. Go down the hall and go inside the door to the left."* He said pointing down the hall.

I walked down the hall and to the door, I read the writing on the door and almost laughed. **ENTER WHEN READY.** As if I could ever be ready for whatever they were going to do to me. I opened the door and walked into the room and saw Andrew dressed in a hazmat suit. *"Ok, now you're starting to worry me. Why is everyone dressed like that?"* I said as I saw him. He just smiled. *"There is nothing to worry about, this is just to keep anything from getting in the room that shouldn't be there. Now we will need you to strip down and head into the glass door you see there for us to begin."* He said pointing at the door, then he left the room.

I stripped down and headed into the small glass box. I closed the door behind me, and just as I closed the door, steam came spraying out from every angle for a few seconds then stopped as the ground pulled everything in. Then it was followed by a two or three-second burst of water sprayed over me. The other end of the box opened and I stepped out into the small room. I looked around the room, and there was nothing but dots on the walls and a chair in the center. *"Well this is seriously creepy don't you think."* Said Peter appearing next to the chair like a TV host showing me my grand prize I had just won.

I walked over to it and sat in the chair, then a metal strap flipped over my arms and legs, now I was getting worried. *"Okay Will we are about to start, now this is not going to hurt so much as it will be uncomfortable. So just bear with it, it will be over in a minute or so* ok." Came the voice of Andrew from all around me. Then the straps tightened, and I felt two needles go into the top of my shoulders, an excruciating feeling, but they shot something into me that soon numbed the pain. Then the small dots all around the room started spraying blue smoke into the chamber filling it completely, I felt the needles jerk back out of me. A minute later the smoke that filled the air disappeared, and I was left sitting in the chair with blue skin.

I stumbled out of the room a bit shaken up by what had just happened. *"That's it, you can go home and get some rest now. Come back in two days to see us, and we can see how everything is going ok."* Said Andrew to me as I walked out of the room looking at my now blue skin, thinking if there was anything I was going to be able to do but sit at home looking like this.

By the time I got home I was ready to pass out, I felt so tired and sleepy, I couldn't believe I wasn't drugged. I got into the room and was thinking maybe I should go and do something maybe try and see if I could figure out my invention, but I didn't even get one foot of my socks off before I was face down in the bed asleep.

Chapter 4

Love is the greatest power

It holds with it mans greatest strength

That is the power to change

Love gives man the power to change everything

To bring about change so great

Even time must step aside for it.

IT WASN'T FATE

The next day I woke up late, after one PM, something I had not done since I was a child. The first thing I did when I woke up was, look in the mirror and saw that I was still a healthy shade of blue, I scream out in shock. Kellie ran into the bathroom to see what was going on, there I was just staring into the mirror at my reflection. *"Relax I know your blue, but they did say they weren't any side effects that lasted more than a day maybe this is one of them."* She said to me in an attempt to calm me down. *"I'm still blue, why am I still blue."* I said with my voice shaking. That whole morning was a strange one, but I felt different from normal, or maybe it was because my skin was blue.

I spent the rest of the day just wondering around the house looking for something to cheer me up. Without my projects, I didn't have anything to distract me from the fact that I was now blue. Not just that but my car design hadn't gotten to the point where they would need my input. I laid around like a slump, while Kellie did her best to cheer me up, but it wasn't working in the least. The next day was the same nothing was different, but the fact that I was still blue.

Three days after I had turned blue, I woke up in the morning and the color was starting to return to my skin, well a not blue color. I headed down to the office with Kellie and as we walked in Andrew was waiting for us. *"Hey, how do you feel Will?"* He said to me as I walked towards him as fast I could so I wasn't outside long, after all, I was still blue. *"I'm doing fine for someone that's blue how do you really think I'm doing!"* I said back to him annoyed at the question. He just laughed and took me to one of the testing rooms that I was used to being in to take blood.

"Okay Will I want you to stop taking everything that you take for MS, we estimated that the treatment will take a week to start working, so if there is no change by then, it means it's not going to work. Oh, and your color should be back by tomorrow." He said with a smile then started to run his test on me for the next hour.

The rest of that week started to go better than I expected, Kellie took the week off from work, and we spent it talking about everything, and even though it hurt it was needed, I felt as if I was finally going to start healing. I even started telling her about my pet project maybe she would see something I didn't and help me figure out what it was. Too bad that it wasn't one of the things that were getting better that week. I felt better than I had in years, and things between Kellie and me were almost back to normal by the end of that week. I was happy as I headed off to sleep that night, I knew that they would be giving me good news in the morning somehow.

The next morning we headed down to the office, I decided that I would drive this time and let Kellie enjoy the ride. We got there and went into the building, expecting Andrew to be waiting for me again, but he wasn't, oddly enough there wasn't anyone at all, not even the regular front desk person. At this point I was a bit scared, my thoughts ran from bad to worst with each moment I didn't see anyone in the building. *"Yep, you're going to die."* Said the voice of Peter out of nowhere.

IT WASN'T FATE

I looked around starting to panic, then a person walked out. *"Oh hey Will, you're here, sorry you must be freaking out. Didn't they call you to tell you not to come today?"* He said walking to me with a sub in his hand. *"No, no one told me anything what's going on here?"* I said confused and in panic. *"Don't worry, its good we got an anonymous donation last week, and now we are moving to a different building."* He said sitting down in the chair behind the desk. *"Oh, here they said to give this to you."* He said taking a letter from the table and holding it out for me to take.

I took the letter and opened it. **Test results from two days after the drug was administered show a 100% restoration of damaged cells including normal cell damage. Further tests will be needed to see if the results will hold up. However, current results show a cure has been found.** I froze letting the letter fall from my hand. *"Oh yeah! Now that's what I'm talking about, it's about time, now watch my feet as I do my happy dance, oh yeah."* Peter said twirling around and moonwalking back and forth in front of me. Kellie picked up the letter expecting something terrible to written on it, her eyes got wide, and she just stopped.

"Yesssss! I can't believe this is happening, please tell me this isn't a joke." I yelled out once I came back to my senses. The guy at the desk looked at me like I had lost my mind. *"Um I don't know what you're talking about, but I need to get going now ok, I was just here to get that letter oddly enough. Now I have to get back and help finish moving."* He said trying to get us out of the building so he could leave or finish

eating.

I got home that day excited about what I had read, my life was going better than I thought possible now. In just a few weeks it had gone from bad to being the best moment of my life, and I knew nothing could make it any better. A thought that made me a bit concerned but at the same time, I didn't care. Andrew called me as I was celebrating at home. *"Oh hey Will I take it you got our letter, well I will see you in a month ok. But if anything happens at all even if you stab your toe give me a call on my cell please."* He said to me sounding a bit odd like something was wrong, but I didn't care. If he wanted to be my personal on-call doctor, I wasn't going to stop him.

A few days later, the partying finally stopped in my head and in my house. I laid in my bed as the day slowly passed by, it was a fantastic day, and I needed to spend it doing something more constructive than sitting in bed. *"Hey Will didn't your first payment from GM clear last week?"* Said Peter standing by the door with something floating in his hands. *"Yeah, it did I almost forgot about that after getting all the good news. Do you think I can get it made now?"* I said then jumped up out of bed and got dressed as fast as I could. I grabbed my flash drive, and I was gone out the door right to my car.

I headed to a small milling shop about an hour drive away. I got there and handed the guy in the shop my flash drive. *"How fast can you have everything on here made. Most of the items are made of titanium, carbon fiber, steel, and harden steel mixed with tungsten."* He took the drive from me and started talking as he walked over to the computer.

"Well, it depends I can have most things made by the next day, but right now they are ten projects in front of yours." He plugged in the flash drive, and the part files stated to roll down his screen. *"But I mean I can always work something out for you if you need it sooner."* I smiled, as his eyes grew wider as he saw the file count. *"Yes, I can most definitely work something out for you sir."* He said again.

"Based on the size of those parts which most of them are actually quite small how fast do you think you can get them all made?" I asked him walking around the shop looking around at everything. *"Well, for the smaller ones I can have up to fifteen of them made at once, but that won't be the big thing it will be the cost some of these materials. They aren't kept in shops. They will have to be ordered specially, so I'm not sure when all of them will be in."* He said to me while writing down notes on a pad. *"Well I want it before the month is over, do what you have to in order to get it done. Anyway, no one sees this design, and I do mean no one."* He looked up from his notes when I said that. *"This isn't dangerous is it?"* He said looking right at me. *"No, well I'm not sure I don't know what it is yet and if it is dangerous, I don't want it getting into the wrong hands."* I talked to him while writing a check.

I handed him the check, and picked up the closed sign from off the counter in front of him. *"I'll be back around midday tomorrow to pick up what you have done already, and that check should cover the cost of the materials. If the work is good, I will pay whatever your normal rate is for manufacturing them upfront."* I said walking over to the door and hanging the sign on it with the closed side facing out. He looked

152

down at the check and then back at me. *"Sir this is too much for just the materials."* He said to me as I was going to open the door. *"An honest man. Not many people like you are left. It's lucky you are too. Take the rest of it as a gift for putting me at the top of your list how's that."* I said then left the store.

I got home that day in a great mood, I walked in and expected to see Kellie happy to see me, but instead, I saw her sitting at the table with an angry look on her face. *"Hey, are you ok?"* I said to her. *"Yeah I'm fine are you, well I bet you are fine not working not doing anything but going out and then getting annoyed with me if I'm not home early."* She said catching me off guard. *"What do you mean, I work and do everything I can for you and..."* She cut me off as I was talking. *"You always do everything right I'm always wrong."* She said then stormed out of the room.

I was lost as to what was going on, everything seemed like it was going perfect the day before and now this. I didn't know what was going on, but I thought she was just mad about something. So I spent the next few days trying to find out what was wrong, but she wouldn't tell me anything that was wrong. Then she started acting like normal again like nothing had happened between us. Now I was utterly lost and confused. A few weeks went by, and it was like nothing had happened, everything seemed great again.

Then the day came for me to go back to see Andrew. I showed up and sat in his office and waited for him to come in, I looked around, and even though it was a new building, nothing had changed same color room and same out of place pictures. He walked into the room all smiles like he had won the lottery. *"Well hello Will, how are you doing. I bet you're doing amazing seeing that you are the first person to be cured of MS."* He said with a smile. *"So it's true then, are we going to do any more test to see what happing."* I said not really knowing what was next after being cured of something. He laughed at me for a bit. *"Yes we have more test to do, and I'm not laughing at you. I just didn't expect you to say the same thing as my assistant."* He said and got up.

I followed him out of the room and into the next one where he ran all the test we would normally run, over the span of a week. First, he took blood samples, then I went into the CAT scan and MRI for a few hours, then more blood was taken. Then after all those tests were done he did the last one, I laid and waited it was the one test I really didn't like doing. I felt his cold hands on my back then a few seconds later, I felt it. The ice-cold needle going into my back and popping into my spine, making a small popping sound that went up my spine into my head and made me almost pass out. After that, I would be staying there that night to rest before I would be heading home.

I left the next morning early to go home. I got home to two packages on the doorstep, from the milling company. I pushed the boxes inside and flopped down in my bed. *"Oh you're not going to put it together, aww come on stop being lazy I would put it together, but we both know why that won't happen."* Said Peter, he pointed at the box rising his eyebrows trying to get me to do what he wanted. After a little while, I got up out of bed. *"Fine, I'll see if I can put it together now leave me alone so I can work on it already."* I said then waved through his body trying to get rid of him. I opened the box expecting ten or twenty parts for me to try and put together and was surprised to find a box filled with pieces. I dumped the pieces out onto my desk and the ground right below it, as I did a note fell from the box. **I have made all but two parts.**

I was soon engulfed with the prospect of putting this thing together, within an hour the whole living room was covered in parts. I inspected each one locking over them and trying to put the pieces where I thought they should go. I got completely lost in what I was doing and didn't notice that Kellie came and went until she messaged me that she was out with her friends.

Chapter 5

Life begins when there is love

From birth we are loved by our parents

Then the rest of our families

We grow older and love more

Bringing new life and new love

Begging the circle of life and love once more.

IT WASN'T FATE

The night passed by before I knew it, I was feeling the rays from the sun hitting my face making me realize that the night was gone. But at least it wasn't a waste, I had done more than I expected to and I was sure I only needed to put a few more pieces on after getting the last two parts. I got up from the desk and got something to eat looked at the time, it was 8 A.M., then I headed off to my room. Kellie shouldn't be waking up for a little while longer seeing that it was now the weekend and she didn't have work. I headed into the room and saw no one was there I looked around a bit and then walked up to the bed.

A sudden shock ran through my body, and I got a headache instantly, I fell forward into the bed and grabbed my head then as suddenly as it came it was gone, leaving me with the strangest feeling of deja vu. *"That was weird, oh well I guess I'm tired, maybe I haven't recovered from the spinal tap yet."* I said aloud to myself as I snuggled up to my pillow.

I woke up when I heard a door close. *"Hello, Kellie is that you?"* I said struggling to fight off the tiredness I was feeling to get up out of bed. *"Yeah, it's me not like you care anyway."* I heard from outside the door. *"Oh ok."* I said falling back into the bed and pulling the sheets close before the words that she said hit me, I jumped up out of bed. *"What was that?"* I said thinking I was dreaming. *"No son, you're not dreaming she is mad."* Peter said shaking his head back and forth sitting on the side of the bed. I jumped up out of bed. *"Shut up you."* I said back to him heading out of the room into the kitchen. She was just sitting watching TV drinking something.

I walked up to her, and before I could say anything, she turned to me. *"You don't love me you just went yeah love you to like I was no one last night."* My mind was lost at that point I had never heard anything like this before, and I had no clue what to say back to her. *"What do you mean? I love you! what are you talking about."* I said to her walking up to her. *"No, you don't you proved that last night, I'm going to stay with my friend tonight."* She said then stormed out of the room and off she went leaving me completely confused as to what was going on, and once again having a feeling of deja vu.

I sat in my chair at my desk completely lost as to what was going on now. *"Well that was new I don't think I have ever heard someone say there is a difference in how you text them you love them before. Maybe she's the one that needs to see someone because that was crazy."* Peter said sitting down in the chair that was now next to me. I turned to him with my mouth opened to say something but I couldn't there were just no words to say at this point. *"Maybe I don't even know what just happened, but where did that chair come from I don't have a second chair."* I said to him. *"Hmm, you don't? That's odd."* He said then as he finished talking the chair vanished from under him letting him fall.

The next week passed by like a blink of an eye, I spent it just waiting around at home watching TV all day. Then I got one message from Kellie, I responded, and she said she wasn't coming back home. I was shocked, but at the same time, I felt a strange feeling of anger and happiness. I couldn't really understand what it was, but I didn't really mind it as much as I expected. I flipped the switch on my desk light for the first time since she left, I looked at the two packages that sat on the table. They held the last two pieces to the machine I was building, they had came during the week, but I didn't open them to see what was in them.

I took the last two pieces out of the boxes and put them where they belonged then fit the final pieces that I had left into it like a puzzle. I didn't know what it was or how it would work because it had no moving parts that ran on any power source. I pushed the button, and nothing happened not even a click. A disappointing moment to say the least. *"Hey, why is that part there hanging off of it?"* Said Peter pointing to the side. I pulled at the piece that was sticking out, and it didn't move, then I pulled the top off and looked inside. I saw what I hoped was the problem. It was one of the magnets that were in it. It was out of place and pulling that other piece out of place. I took the magnet out and pushed the pieces back into place. Then I lined the magnet up with the center and dropped it in.

It fell in and stopped just before it would touch anything and started wobbling. I quickly put on the top and looked into the small hole at the side, and watched as the magnet started spinning, then slowly stopped just floating in the center. Then something I didn't expect happened, the box-shaped of the machine started to change as everything started pulling into the center. A few seconds later and it was a perfect sphere with four one inches holes opposite each other on it. I looked into the hole, and it went straight through to the other side.

IT WASN'T FATE

"Hold on a minute don't touch it yet." Peter's voice said as he grabbed my hand stopping me right before I touched it. **SNAP!**

The sound rang through the room as the sphere flew to the wall and slammed into it. I heard a humming sound, the lights dimmed then flickered and went out. Then my computer screen just shut off, I backed up slowly as the sphere started surging with electrical energy. *"No way man, you made an electrical magnet. Do you know how much havoc this thing could cause?"* Peter said to me laughing and jumping up and down. *"I don't think that's what it is, it has too many parts for that, it's as if this is how it gets the power it needs for something else."* I said looking around as everything in my house went off one by one in order of how far away they were from the sphere. *"Well I think you should shut it down for now, don't you think."* Peter said to me. *"Yeah, I think that would be a good idea now I just hope that's what the button on it does."* I said poking at it with a plastic spoon trying to push the button. **CLICK**

I managed to push the button, nothing happened at first, but just as I was going to start freaking out it just fell off the wall, and everything turned back on. *"Well that was interesting, but I don't know how soon I will be turning this thing back on again."* I said looking at Peter, who was just all smiles. *"What are you talking about you did see that thing right."* Replied Peter full of excitement. I picked it up off the ground and looked it over, I needed to know what it was. They were so many parts in it, and most of them didn't move, but after seeing it run, I was starting to get an idea of what it did. If I was correct, it was pulling all the electricity into itself towards the magnet in the center. And all the small pieces in it would do something once that energy had built up enough. But what I didn't understand was the need for the four holes, and what it did after it had enough power.

I laid back in the chair holding it above my head, staring at it wondering what was going to happen when it had the power it needed. I looked down, and my phone rang it had a new message. **I sent you the divorce papers just sign them.** It was a message from Kellie that left me a bit more than hurt that she would just up and leave. I wanted to say something back so badly, but I couldn't bring myself to do it instead I just sat there with the phone in my hand. *"I think you should call Andrew, Will."* Peter said to me breaking the silence in my head. *"What why would I do that, it's not like he's my close friend or anything."* I said back to him. *"Yeah, but your nose is bleeding so maybe you should call him."* As Peter spoke, I realized that the warm feeling on my lips was blood, and that I wasn't smelling the metal from the sphere but from my blood. *"What do you care anyway? You're not even real."* I said annoyed and on the brink of crying. He looked over at me without his usual smile. *"I live here too you know, now call him before I make you."* He said snapping me out of the depressed state I was in long enough to make the call.

I sat and thought about everything that was going on in my life as I waited for Andrew to show up. I hadn't fully accepted what had happened the week before between Kellie and me until this point and now it was crashing me as the thoughts ran through my mind. What

161

would I do now what was things going to be like from this point on, was I just doomed to be alone from now on? I just sat and let the bad thoughts flow through my head filling it up completely, making me feel as if I deserved to die.

Knock Knock. Came from the door and I slowly went to answer it. I opened the door, and Andrew took one look at me. *"You're coming with me now."* He said and pulled me out of the door, helping me to his car. Before I knew it, I was in a room laying on a bed with machines all around me monitoring me. A nurse walked into the room that I recognized somehow. *"What happened why am I here?"* I said to her as she walked up to my bed. *"Well Dr. Andrew brought you in sedated, he said to make sure you got some rest and see if there was anything wrong with you."* She said back to me. I closed my eyes and laid back. *"Well it doesn't matter what's wrong with me, I've lost the will to live ironic right? Seeing that everyone calls me Will."* I said with an angry sarcastic tone of voice. She just laughed at me. *"Oh by the way my name is Nafisa I'll be your nurse for now, but I don't think you will be here too long."* She smiled and then walked out of the room.

Act 5

Chapter 1

Love and time together

They can bend anything to there will

Apart they are weak

Causing a longing for love

And longing for more time

But when they are found together

They stop all other thought

Existing forever in love in an instant that spans all of time.

IT WASN'T FATE

I spent a week in the hospital, Andrew made sure I was kept there by telling the doctors I was a danger to myself because of the experimental drug I had taken. He was not going to let me go home and be alone until he was sure I was over Kellie. I laid in the bed with nothing to do. I couldn't bring my computer in the room because I could break it and use it to hurt myself. Even though I was over giving up on life by the second day, he wasn't taking any chances.

Every day I would wake up and wait for Nafisa to come and take my vitals then wait so I could take a shower, seeing that I wasn't allowed in the bathroom without someone nearby. I would spend the whole time I was in the shower talking about something. So she could make sure I wasn't doing something else, and by the third day, I had actually started to feel much better. Having someone listen to everything I said was a bit of a change for me, especially when it came to my personal life.

Six days of this did even more than I expected and made me feel much better than I had thought I would be able to feel for a long time to come. For some reason, I started to feel great sitting in my bed waiting for her shift to start, waiting for when she would come in, and I would get to talk to her. But I was disappointed as a different person came that day. *"Hey I'm Paul, go shower and count out loud for me."* He said to me, then unlocked the door and sat in the chair next to it with a book.

The next day I slept in, I knew I was getting out that day, and I doubt that they would send anyone to stay in my room that day. *"Why aren't you awake yet, I have a schedule to keep you know. Come on get* up." Nafisa's voice said as she shook me in the bed waking me up. *"Why are you here?"* I said to her as she headed to the door and unlocked it. *"I know you miss me, now come entertain me with your weird life."* She said then sat down and folded her legs with a smile point at the door.

Though I was happy that she came, I was also a bit sad because I knew this would be my last time talking to her. *"Hey I know I shouldn't ask this, but I don't really care at this point seeing that it's the last time you will be out there doing this anyway."* I said getting into the shower. *"What's that you're saying, you think you're leaving?"* She said giggling under her voice. *"Yes I'm leaving, and well I was wondering if well you know."* She interrupted me. *"No, I don't know. Now hurry up I'm late now because you wanted to sleep in."* She said to me, I was nervous now and I paused I didn't know what to say. I shut off the shower and got out. But she was gone, I had missed my chance to say anything to her all because I slept late. *"Ha Ha, you suck you know that, I can't believe you didn't get her number. What a loser you are it's sad that I live in your body."* Peter said standing at the door dressed as a doctor.

Just as I opened my mouth to speak Andrew walked into the room. *"Hey Will I'm going to sign the papers so that you can leave, so please don't do anything to hurt yourself. Oh before I forget can you come in tomorrow so I can run a test it should be the last one before I have all the data to go public with the cure."* He said to me, then he handed me the clipboard he had in his hands for me to sign. After I signed he left without another word, he just gave me a creepy look to say that he was watching me.

IT WASN'T FATE

I was soon packing up my things to leave, I was ready to get out of this place after I failed to talk to Nafisa that morning. I didn't have much of anything to pack up, just two shirts Andrew had brought me. I sat on the side of the bed with the small bag in my hands and looked at the food that I was supposed to eat for breakfast. I pulled the tray to myself, took the drink off the plate, and started to drink it. I finished it and went to put it back and pick up the napkin next to it to wipe my mouth. Right as the napkin reached my mouth, I noticed a black spot. *"Aww come on a dirty napkin as if I wasn't unlucky enough today already."* I said and threw the napkin down onto the tray it hit the cup of coffee on the tray and dropped in. The napkin started to absorb the coffee, and I noticed that it had words written on it. I grabbed it pulling it out before the coffee hit the writing. **I knew you wouldn't ask so here's my number.**

I knew it was from Nafisa the second I saw it. *"Oh now your all smiles thinking you got game now don't you. Well, guess what you have no game, she's the one with game, such a sad fact."* Peter said looking at me with a look of disappointment, that you would give a dog not bringing back anything when trying to play fetch. I pushed the napkin in my pocket before replying to him. *"Shut up you before I start thinking about you in a pink tutu."* The look on his face changed to one of horror, then he shook his head. *"You wouldn't."* I just smiled and hummed waiting for them to say I could go.

I called her that night, and she picked up the phone catching me by surprise. I had fully expected her to give me a fake number or not answer at all if it was her number. But instead, what happened was much more surprising than her answering. She answered, and we talked and talked about everything that came to mind for hours on end. Before we knew it, the sun was starting to shine through the windows. At that point, we had to call it a night or really morning and try to get some sleep before we would have to get back to our daily lives. As I laid there trying to fall asleep, I couldn't help but think this was what I wanted from my life. I had everything else, but now I had a friend I could talk to about anything.

Andrew called me soon after I had fallen asleep to come to his office so he could do the last few tests and talk to me about everything that I had gone through, then what would be happening next. I arrived at his office and went in. *"Hey Will, just sit for a bit I have a few more things to write down, and then we can get everything started."* Andrew said to me writing in a file folder he had in his hands. *"It's okay whenever you're ready, I have all day."* I replied to him closing my eyes as I laid back in the chair.

"Ok well, that finishes up my work now it's time we talked about why I wanted you to come in." He said after a few minutes getting up and pulling gloves out of the box on the small table next to him. *"Well, first off everything was a success however, I haven't told you much about anything this whole time. So first I would like to start with the test drug you took."* He said snapping the gloves on and bring a needle close to my arm to take blood. *"I'm sure the first thing about it you must be wondering is why you were blue for two days. And well its cause we dyed you blue. I know it sounds like we just did it for no reason and*

honestly, it really didn't have a reason besides the fact that we died the drug that was sprayed into the air blue to ensure we didn't use the wrong one. But it also helped you not go outside. Which was great because the drug sprayed onto your skin was meant to keep you from sweating out the actual drug we injected into you." He finished talking as he spun his chair around with the two blood samples he had just taken from my arm.

"You know you're not making this sound very good." I sad as I pulled my sleeve back down. *"Well, I don't really care. I cured you so get over It."* He said spinning back around laughing. *"I'm just kidding with you. So here's the part that was really important. Remember the two needles that went into your shoulders. They were the key to this whole thing and honestly, something that we thought wouldn't work at all. I was honestly hoping you would just get a little better, not end up completely curing and all the damage to your brain to heal."* Andrew said as he spun around again and started looking through some papers he had with him. He pulled one out and handed it to me then started to talk again.

"You see what was in those needles was actually something that we tried before. The first was a compound that helps coat fat cells, and the other was basically just a super cocktail of everything the brain and nervous system needs to build a whole new one. With that, the body started to heal itself but then something we didn't expect happened, the two started working together and the first bonded with the second and just filled in the damaged areas in the cells. Causing all the damage

in your brain to be repaired overnight, including the normal damage from aging and any injury you ever had. Right now your brain is actually the healthiest in the world." He finished talking, and I was lost he had handed me two MIRs, and I didn't know what they meant.

"What's this? You know I'm not a doctor right I can't read this you do know that right?" I said to him turning the paper on its side then flipping it the other way and holding it up to the light. *"Yes I know but it's labeled before and after, look at the color of the before, the blue is the parts of your brain that are working at the best possible functionality. Now, look at the after image and the difference between the two."* He said smiling a huge smile filled with pride. The before image only had a small amount of it that was blue and in the after image everything was blue. *"Okay, I see it. I get it. What's your point?"* I asked, he just smile and handed me another paper. I looked at it, it was another MRI, but this one had a few images of MRIs on it. *"Those are MRIs of some of the healthiest and smartest people in the world, and none of them have half their brains working at its best. The thing is we think that the only time the brain functions at its best, is in the first few years of life when the body is still in the building stages."* He said laying back with a smile that just screamed he wasn't telling me everything.

"Okay, I know there's something you aren't telling me now." I said as I looked at him lost as to what all this meant. *"You don't see it yet do you?"* He said looking at me curiously as to why I didn't understand him. *"Your brain has been reset to what it was as a child. The parts of your brain that control building your body have been turned back on. In*

other words, your internal clock has been reset to zero, and your body is rebuilding itself like new." I looked at him wondering what it meant, I didn't know if he was saying I no longer had to take anything or I was going to need it again. Then he just started laughing and shaking his head, then stood up and shook my hand. "*Will I'm telling you, you're the first person to drink from the fountain of youth.*" I looked at him confused for a moment. "*No, I don't want to live in this body forever. Nooo, I hate you.*" Peter said appearing behind Andrew in all black.

"*Nah I'm kidding man, its party time!*" Peter said again with a smile and fireworks going off behind him, dancing and fading back into nothingness.

I stayed frozen for a few minutes as what Andrew said set in. "*Well we aren't sure as of yet what kind of side effects this will have on the body but, you can still get hurt and die you just won't age or die naturally anymore we think.*" Andrew said then walked out of the room leaving me lost.

Chapter 2

The hands of time tick and tock away

Bring life with each movement of its cosmic hands

Getting stronger, weaker, smaller, and larger

Creating new bonds with each tick

That grows into love at each tock

The love that allows the hands to move.

I got home that day and laid in my bed lost in thought, I stared into the device I had made as my mind wandered, thinking about what I was going to do and if Andrew was telling me the truth about no longer aging. My eyes closed and my thoughts went to Kellie, and what had happened between us then it wondered to Nafisa for some reason. I opened my eyes, and everything went black, then I was sitting in a house that for some reason seemed very familiar but at the same time, it was completely unknown to me. I turned, and I saw a wedding picture, in it was Crystal and me kissing at the altar. Then suddenly I was back in my room.

I dropped the sphere and jumped up looking around, that couldn't be a dream I was awake, and that was nothing like any of the hallucinations I have ever had. It felt like a memory, and it felt like a memory of something that happened the day before. *"Hey Will you okay you don't look that great."* Peter said standing next to me. I looked over at him. *"Phil is that you?"* I said confused by what I was saying. *"Well I haven't heard that name in a while, I'm surprised you still remember it."* Peter replied to me. My head started to pound as I opened my mouth, I fell back and sat on the bed holding my head.

"Why did I call you Phil, who is Phil anyway?" I said to Peter who just looked at me and shrugged his shoulders. *"Beats me but that's not what's important right now. I think you should call Andrew."* I laid back down on the bed for a few minutes before getting up and getting some water and calling Andrew to talk to him. He told me the headaches

were normal, and the flash I had about Crystal was normal for someone under as much stress as I was. Then he proceeded to tell me how I should be doing fun things seeing that I had so much money.

Well, I took Andrews advice and booked a flight to leave the next day to someplace across the planet. Then I called Nafisa. *"Hey, I know this is weird but do you want to go on a trip tomorrow?"* I asked as soon as she picked up the phone. *"Wow, really you want to take me on a trip now, well you know money isn't going to buy me, but I'll still go."* She replied. *"Ha ha very funny, who even said I wanted to buy you, I just want a nurse with me in case I do something stupid."* I said back to her laughing. *"What you're not serious are you?"* She said back as I just laughed and told her bye.

I headed into the next room with my device in my hand, wondering why I had made this thing. I flopped down on the couch and then flipped on the TV. As soon as I turned it on, I saw the strangest blue light swirling around on it almost as if the TV was just behind the light, then it was just gone. *"That was weird must have been something with the power for the TV."* I said out loud flipping the channels. *"Yeah, sure whatever you say Will. But I have a question for you why are you holding that thing if you don't know what it does."* Peter said to me, I looked down and realized that my fingers were in the holes on the sphere without me even realizing it. *"I don't know I just feel like I'm missing something important about it."* I said flipping more channels looking for something interesting.

A few minutes passed, and I couldn't find anything to watch, so I flipped off the TV and head to my porch to get some fresh air. I looked out over the grass, and to the lake that was behind the buildings I lived in. I stared into the blue waters of the lake and wondered if anything in my life had really changed since I had moved into this place. I stayed out on the porch pondering my life for a few hours before I realized I needed to pack for the next day.

The morning came faster than I expected it to, I headed down to the airport and met up with Nafisa. We boarded the plane, I felt a bit weird sitting next to her on the plane when I was technically still married, but that was just until the paperwork went through. However, this didn't seem to matter after the plane took off, me and Nafisa were talking, and we didn't stop the whole twelve hours we were in the air. By the time the plane touch down, we must have told each other everything in our lives.

But what happened on the trip, I didn't see coming in the least. We bonded like I had never done with anyone before, I told her everything about myself, all of my hopes, fears, and dreams. She was my best friend by the time we got back on the plan three days later. The plane took what seemed like a few minutes to fly the twelve-hour flight as we talked.

I dropped her off at her place, and I walked her to her door. I give her a hug and as I was about to turn she gave me a kiss on the forehead. *"Thank you Will, I had a great time. I don't think I have ever been this close to any of my friends in my life."* She said to me as she walked into her door.

IT WASN'T FATE

"Wow you're her friend, man you have negative game at this point, I think I have a better chance with her, and she can't even see me." Peter said sitting in the seat next to me as I drove home. *"What, I like it this way I don't think I should be in anything with anyone after what happened with Kellie and the strange things that I've been going through lately. I just don't think I could handle falling in love again right now anyway."* I said to him. *"Aww what a wimp you are, you know that right?"* Peter said back to me. After that, we drove just listening to the radio the rest of the way home.

I laid in my bed looking at the ridges in the ceiling plaster, rolling the sphere around on my chest thinking about what it might be used for. **CLICK.** *"Ahh."* I yelled out jumping up as the sphere clipped a piece of my skin off. It hit the corner of the room and rolled off to a wall socket. *"No No No No!"* I yelled as I jumped off the bed towards it to try to grab it off the wall before it started pulling power. I stopped midair as the sphere began to glow, then a bolt of electricity shot out from it right into my eyes and everything just stopped. I felt a strange feeling of warmth then a sudden pull from behind me almost as if I was being pulled and stuffed into something.

A sudden shock ran through my body, and I got a massive headache instantly, I fell forward into the bed and grabbed my head then as suddenly as it came it was gone, leaving me with the strangest feeling of deja vu. *"That was weird, oh well I guess I'm tired, maybe I haven't recovered from the spinal tap yet."* I said out loud to myself as I snuggled up to my pillow.

IT WASN'T FATE

My eyes opened back. *"Wait a minute what just happened why did I just say that."* I said jumping off the bed and looking around frantically. *"Hey relax man you had a Spinal tap yesterday take it easy."* I instantly blacked out as I heard those words.

Chapter 3

The time has come once again to love

Once again to be loved

Once again to be needed

Once again to need another

The time has come once again

Love has come once again

And with it fate is sealed.

IT WASN'T FATE

"Do you know how long you were out?" Said Peter, as I opened my eyes. *"I don't know, how long has it been?"* I asked him as I sat up. *"Why are you asking me? How should I know how long you were out? I was gone too you know."* Peter replied to me, with his ear to ear smile on his face. I got up and headed to my computer to check the time, I saw the date and time and froze. This couldn't be real it was three days after my spinal tap, if this date was correct the time at the hospital my trip, it all never happened. I looked around and grabbed my phone, I called up Crystal. She was the first person that came to mind for some strange reason.

The phone call between Crystal and me was very short, but she confirmed my fears that the time was correct. Somehow I had found a way back in time which by all I knew should be impossible, well it couldn't be possible, then I looked over my desk and saw it, the device I had made was now back to what it was that day missing two pieces. Everything was going exactly the same as it did the last time, I was reliving my life at home alone. But this time I spent the time looking up every theory of time travel I could find. Then when I couldn't find anything, I finish putting together the device to get my mind off of things.

It snapped and then hit the wall glowing like before. Just like before I reached for it to get it off the wall but as my hand reached it I was back in my room with my head pounding, then **BOOM!** I hit the ground, and the sphere fell in front of me. I looked around the room wondering if I had jumped into the future where I started. I got up, ran to my computer, and checked the date, it was the day I came back from my trip. It was then I knew beyond doubt that what had happened was not a dream, it was real, it had to be real. I looked over the sphere after I got back to my room, but it didn't make sense that this small thing could do anything to allow me to travel in time. Maybe this was just a strange side effect of the drug, but I couldn't help but believe it wasn't.

I sat at my computer desk reading article after article about time travel, but everything I read was all hopeless. It showed no ways for it to be possible. I knew that the sphere I made couldn't send me through time all it did was pull energy into itself storing it in a physical form. Which in itself was amazing but at the same time was very dangerous, considering that the physical form of energy was extremely unstable. Not only was it unstable it was also on the break of being released all at once as soon as the device stopped holding it in. This device couldn't allow for time travel. However, from what I had read about time travel a device like this would be needed to power whatever was send me back in time. From that day on, I made it my mission to find out what happened to me and how it is that I jumped back in time or if I was just going even further off the deep end.

Even though I devoted all my free time to figuring out what happened to me that day, I still found time to enjoy my life. My search for an answer was stressful and almost maddening because no matter how far I went I was still nowhere, not only that, but it was consuming my mind with each day. Luckily, I kept talking to Nafisa about it, and over the months that turned into years, she was there for me preventing me from going over that edge of insanity.

Years passed by as I searched for my answer to what happened that day. My life in those years changed more than any one person's life might have ever changed in history. I created the most amazing technology in my search to understand what happened that day. Starting with Antigravity platforms that made space travel an everyday thing. Then I moved on to turning the device I created into an energy source that drew energy directly off of anything. With it, power plants no longer lose energy at transformer stations, but the main thing it allowed for was effortless power generation from heat. As my work started to change the face of the planet, I funded Andrews's research, and five years after that fateful day, the cure to life was announced with me at the center of attention.

The next five years changed the world, and something no one expected happened. An unexpected side effect from the drug was infertility, with the drug reverting the brain to perfect form and causing the body to undergo radical regenerations it caused the reproductive system to no longer produced Eggs or Sperm. It wasn't just a side effect, it was a message sent from God not to tamper in his domain. But it was a message overlooked by the masses as most took the drug because they valued their life over having children.

Chapter 4

Tick tock goes the clock

Tap tap goes the steps

Thump thump goes the heart

Silence

The sound the love makes

So loud it overpowers all

Yet so quite it can only be heard but by two.

IT WASN'T FATE

"How long have we know each other now, it's been almost fifty years hasn't it." I said turning to Nafisa. *"Yeah I think so, that sounds about right."* She replied to me sitting on the sofa flipping channels. *"I have never seen you on a date in all that time. Why is that?"* I asked her, she paused for a moment. *"Well, why are you still in this same small apartment even though you could buy this country if you wanted to."* She replied to me completely ignoring the question. *"Well not because I have money doesn't mean I should waste it I do employ over twenty thousand people you know."* I said back to her walking over with a bowl of popcorn.

I froze not knowing what to say back to her for a moment. *"I love you too."* Was all that came out of my mouth before I could think of what to say. She moved over, laid against me, and took some of the popcorn. *"I know you do, but I love you more."* She replied as she stopped on one of the shows she liked to watch. *"Your welcome."* Said Peter who appeared next to me on the arm of the sofa. *"You can thank me later by the way."* He continued then vanished just as quickly as he had came. That night she fell asleep in my arms on the sofa, something she had done many times before but this time it felt different.

As Nafisa slept that night I couldn't sleep, my mind just kept racing. I had spent so much time working on a way to go back in time, but gave up on it when it looked like I was going to finally crack it. But now I had a reason to finish it I was going to do something I should have done many years ago. I headed to my desk, which hadn't changed a bit since I first started working on projects. I picked up a small round coin-like object and placed it on the back of my neck. *"Engage neural link, projection mode."* I spoke out loud then the coin lit up red, blue, then green. The desk in front of me opened up, and the ground moved forward with the chair I was in as the ground under where the desk was opened.

I stood up as the ground stopped moving, then lights came on in a massive room. A round tall cylinder rolled up next to me then opened, inside was a white robot with no features. *"Wake up its time to get to work."* I said walking away from the robot in the cylinder, Peter appeared in front of me looking at me with his gigantic smile on his face. *"Oh stop acting like you're the boss of me."* He said walking over to the robot and stepping into it. The robot shock then stepped out of the cylinder as a hologram of Peter appeared around it.

"To think you kept this place hidden from everyone for almost forty years, you know you're one of a kind." Said Peter from the robot body, walking up to one of the tables with a screen on it. *"I am glad I made this thing. To think there is a way to allow my subconscious to manifest in a full physical form. Thanks to this handy little thing I get to work 24 hours a day even while I sleep right Peter."* I said looking over at Peter with a smile. *"Ha ha, that's very funny. You make me work while you sleep all night, you're like a slave master I hate you sometimes."* He replied to me as he pulled up the research and old designs that we used to work on.

The whole room lit up as blue lines filled the room and projected

3D designs, and line drawings appeared all over the room. *"Let's get to work now."* I said, as I turned my chair around and rolled over to the other table. We got to work from that point until I couldn't stay awake anymore, at that point, I headed off to sleep as Peter worked on finishing up a design we had started years ago.

By morning, the design was done, and my 3D printing system was building the parts for it. I looked over at the first device I had created, I knew somehow it had something to do with me traveling through time, but I just couldn't figure out just how it was used for the travel. I then spent the next few days working on the problem at hand. However my mind wasn't fully on my time travel problem, some of it was thinking about Nafisa. Though we saw each other every day, we didn't talk about what happened or that much for that matter. There was this strange feeling between us, as if nothing needed to be said for us to understand each other. The next few weeks went by in no time at all, I wanted so badly to tell her I wanted to be with her, but I had wasted so much time not telling her being afraid of love or something else.

As time went by I soon reached a bump, or so it seemed at first. I had found something promising that lead me to believe I had found a way back in time after all. But the problem was there was no way to tell when or where I would end up. Which I knew I wouldn't be able to ignore, a blind jump through time would be a risk too high to take, if I couldn't figure out something to allow me to control my jump. I rolled the sphere I had created so long ago around in my hands wondering what to do. I knew something controlled my jump back then, how else would I be pulled back to the same instant I left.

"*Hey, maybe it's the power.*" Said Peter, to me appearing next to me sitting on the desk. "*Of course it's the power source, what else would it be?*" I replied to him. "*That's not what I meant, I mean it's the power source that's directing the control of the time jump.*" He said with a smile. It hit me soon after how much sense it made, I was trying to find a way to fix the system to allow me to control the time jump when the system already had a way to be controlled built into it by its very design. But now the problem was figuring out how to activate it and how the power controlled the jump. "*Here's an idea why don't you active it, like you did the last time.*" It seemed as though the jump had a limited time for the jump before I was pulled back to my body, or at least that's how I thought it worked.

I headed into my lab and set up the device I had made with the original one then I let it draw power from my grid. I did my best to limit the amount of energy the system gave off as too not allow too much power to go into the machine. Then I used the new part I had created to control and direct the energy in an attempt to cut a hole in time.

Day after day, I spent hours trying to activate the system, but nothing would work, all I would get were shots, or feedback, or huge blots of energy shooting everywhere. I decided to take one last try this time with twice the energy, and I would let it absorb it all at once before trying to turn on anything.

I flipped the power switch and waited until everything in the lab went out then I reached for the power switch to the devices. I hit the switch, and the power was redirected then **BOOM**. Two huge bolts of lightning came shooting out from the machine. One hit the wall, and the other came right at me hitting me right in my face.

I jumped up screaming, looking around everywhere. I must have been dreaming I thought as I got up off the bed and opened the door. *"Hey Will how did you sleep."* Said Nafisa from the kitchen. She was making pancakes something she only did once a week, which was odd seeing that she made them two days ago when she came over. I walked to the kitchen, and I heard something on the TV that caught my attention. I turned to see the comical about a special one-time deal at the park the next day. I quickly turn to the digital calendar on the fridge and saw the date. It was three days earlier it worked. *"Yesss! It worked."* I yelled out in the kitchen, Nafisa looked at me confused. *"Oh sorry I just thought of something for a new idea is all."* I said to her and walked over to grab the plates like I did the last time only to trip and realize I was back in my lab again.

Chapter 5

Tick tick goes the hands of time

Forever marching forward towards the end

Getting ever closer as it ticks

It approaches the end of its journey

Then as it ticks to its end it begins again

Down a path it has traveled many times before

Yet this is a new path never traveled before.

IT WASN'T FATE

It took me a few minutes to get my balance back after the jump. *"Peter do you know what just happened. And why do I feel like your name isn't Peter."* I said with a smile then started laughing. *"Oh yeah we did it now it's time to see how it worked."* He said jumping and celebrating with me. After a few minutes of dancing and celebrating, I set up the machine once again for another jump this time I would use even more power and see if I would stay longer.

CLICK. The machine clicked and sent out a bolt of energy right at my head, however this time I didn't try to avoid it I figured my body was being sent back in time by the bolt or it just wasn't hitting me, either way, I would be fine. Everything went dark for a moment then I opened my eyes at the computer desk. I looked down at the desk at the time on the screen. Two and a half weeks this time. This time I need to see what was happening and if I was really going back in time. But I was alone at home, so I flipped on the computer and wrote a note that just had the time and date in it, then I saved it as **TJ** and put it in a folder I never used. Then set the alarm for ten minutes. I would write the time in it along with something else I thought up.

I coughed as my head pounded for a few minutes as I returned to my regular time. I went on the computer and read the note I left to myself, I knew I didn't make it to the ten minutes, but the file wasn't opened until that day. The realization of what was actually going on didn't fully hit me, but it was close. I knew now that I could affect the past, but I only had a short time to do it. I took a break for a little while then I measured the amount of energy I used with each jump versus how far back I went. From that, I was almost sure I figured out how to determine how far back in time I would go, but not where I would go. It seemed as though I appeared someplace in the house all the time. I was going to do another jump, I would be more careful and try to stay longer.

I had a theory, about how the time limit worked, seeing that I always showed up in my house and I never once saw myself from that time period, it meant that I was only able to stay there until I was close to myself. Then I would be pushed out of that instant in time back to my own right before we came in contact with each other. Which makes perfect sense, seeing that I wasn't from that time, I would get pushed out once the atoms in my body came to close to the atoms in my body of the earlier version. That would prevent the same atoms from two different times from meeting in one place. To avoid that and test to see if I understood how this worked I would try and jump back to when I was out of the state a month earlier.

CLICK. My head pounded like never before, everything staying black for a few seconds longer than usual. As I got my vision back, I saw something I didn't expect, it was the hotel I stayed in. This couldn't be right, or maybe it was perfect. I ran to the bathroom, and I saw it, a small cut I had gotten from shaving the day before I left for the trip. At that moment, the full realization of what was going on hit me. I wasn't sending my body back in time, I was sending my mind back in time. That explained everything. *"Peter are you here or is it just my conscience* *that came back in time."* He appeared in front of me. *"No, it's your whole mind that gets sent back, but for how long?"* He said with a smile from ear to ear that almost pulled his face into it. *"I think it's only five minutes or so at a time, but it is going to be hard to change anything in just five minutes, this might have been a waste after all."* I said to Peter.

Soon after I was back in my lab, I knew now what the machine really did. It gathered up energy and then punched a hole back in time and pushed my mind through it back in time temporarily. Maybe it could even maintain a link with my mind of the present with the one in the past, which could explain the time limit. The system must only have enough power left over to hold the link open for five minutes before it shut down and the link to my past self was cut suddenly.

I spent the next two months jumping back in time to different periods in my life over the past ten years. Figuring out exactly how the system worked and learning more about how I could change time with each jump. I even managed to figure out how to do single shot jumps from one time to another when the time limit ended without returning to my normal time.

After the first two months, I noticed that nothing had changed, every time I jumped back in time I managed to do absolutely nothing. I never said anything to anyone while back in time because there was either no one around or there was too much pain from the jump to remember what I was going to say before I was pulled back to my time. Which started to drive me a bit insane, day after day I would make jumps going back further each time. But no matter what I did, I never had an effect on anything, and I started to believe that there was no way to change time. It just seemed like time found a way for everything to happen the same way no matter what I did.

Before I realized it, ten years had passed, and I had visited almost every point in my life. Well, any that I thought had any impact on my life anyway, then I remembered something. That dream I had about Crystal that seemed so real and familiar had happened to me once before. And I knew exactly what date it was too. I wanted to see what happened that day I was blacked out maybe I would go back just before it happened in the afternoon then work my way forward seeing what happened that day why I had that strange dream or whatever it was.

The machine charged and shot the bolt of energy out at me hitting me right in the face knocking me back, for a moment I didn't feel anything, I opened my eyes to see my lab and everything in it frozen. Something that had never happened and was about to worry me when I felt the pull of being sent back in time, grab me with more force than ever before. I was ripped out of my body and pulled back, it felt like I was riding a roller-coaster strapped to the front of the car. Then I felt myself being pulled apart right at the moment I saw through the eyes of my past self. But what I saw wasn't that day or any day of my life. It was just a glimpse, but what I saw wasn't even a place on this planet it just couldn't be, then I heard my voice coming from all around me. *"Well, it's about time you got this far."*

Then I was back in my body lying on the floor of my lab, my head pounding as if I just got shot in the head, with blood running down from my nose. I couldn't even move to get up for quite some time, and when I did finally manage to move, I was only able to make it to the table. Which had my link on it to allowing Peter to control his robot body and help me up and into my room so I could lay in bed. I started to black out, and for the first time Peter lost control of the robot body, it hit the ground, and I was gone soon after.

"What the hell! Wake up what did you do to yourself." I heard Nafisa yell at me waking me up from one of the strangest dreams I had ever had in my life. I turned to her, but when I opened my eyes, I was lost at what I saw. It was her, Crystal and Kellie for a moment all saying the same thing then I blacked out again.

I woke up in the hospital a week later, I saw Nafisa lying next to me when I opened my eyes. *"What happened?"* I said nudging her to wake up, she looked up at me. *"What happened is I'm going to kill your butt for scaring me like that. The doctors said you had a shock to your system with more power that they had ever seen anyone endure, they don't even know how you lived."* She said angrily staring right into my eyes. *"Sorry but it's not what you think, so come on stop with the pointy face you know I can't take anything you say seriously when you make that face."* I said to her with a smile trying to calm her down, but she wasn't having it. Then she pulled my neural link from her bag. *"And what is this thing and why was it stuck to your neck when I found you."* She said folding her hands.

I took it from her hand and put it on my neck. *"I'll show you, turn on the TV."* She looked at me angrily but then turned on the TV. I activated the link and Peter appeared on the screen. *"Oh, hey it's nice to finally meet you Nafisa, I mean it's about time you let her see me after everything."* He said to her waving and smiling. *"That's Peter he's well I'm not sure how to explain him, but he appeared when I first got sick and just never went away. This coin is my neural link I designed it to allow him to interact with the physical world, it hacks into any nearby computer system, then controls it to project my subconscious onto it which as far as I can tell he lives in and controls most of."* I explain to her as Peter made a fool of himself changing into random clothes and smiling his huge face swallowing smile.

After showing her Peter, I spent the rest of my stay at the hospital explaining to her what I was doing all this time and why I never left the apartment. Some of which went over well with her while a lot of it she either didn't understand or didn't like. I was allowed to leave the hospital that day and head home. Nafisa made sure to lock me in my room and keep my link out of reach when I got home.

After being asleep for a whole week, I didn't want to sleep anymore, and I started to think back to the jump. My head started hurting as I began to remember what happened, and then a flood of memories came rushing back to me. Memories of being married to Crystal and Memories of things I did with Kellie that never happened, well to my knowledge they didn't happen, and they didn't make sense. *"Peter your name is Phil, you were from one of my books."* He appeared in front of me on the edge of the bed, he was almost scary this time. He turned to me slowly, and chills went down my spine as I saw the front of his head missing his face, then his huge smile just appeared across his face and nothing else, then his smile shrunk and the rest of his face appeared.

"So you finally remember, don't you? It's about time I thought I was never going to be able to stop acting like you didn't go messing around with the past." His voice didn't have the normal cartoon-like voice that I was use to, but at the same time, I knew it was the same Peter. "So now you remember that you have been messing around with time for a few hundred years now, tell me are you going to keep doing it or are you happy with this timeline." He said seeming more like himself as his smile started to grow bigger. "Well I don't really remember all that much to be honest just Crystal, and the changes I made with Kellie." I said to him. "Well that is most of it, hmm let's see you have divorced Crystal a total of seventy-five times and a total of sixty times from Kellie. Each time you found a way back in time and change the timeline to fix the mistake you made, but somehow it still ends. Honestly, I don't know how you did it after the tenth time I would've given up on love." Peter replied to me.

That night I learned a lot about myself and time as a whole. I had been traveling back in time for more than a hundred lifetimes all in an effort to fix the mistakes I made. Over that time, I managed to shape the world I needed to help me with my endeavor. Everything from the jobs, Kellie, and crystal had to the cure to life and many of the significant advances in technology across the whole planet. With the ability to travel back in time I had no limit on what I could accomplish and be a part of for that matter. Even getting my first deal with GM was all caused by me going back in time and sending the design to the head of the engineering departments personal email address that I had received after getting the deal with them.

However, I found out that I had been tampering with time for far too long, and if I kept it up, I would risk destroying myself and everyone whose life I had an effect on. *"So tell me, how many times have I jumped back in time?"* I asked Peter, his smile went right back to touching his ears. *"Twenty-two million and five times."* I paused for a minute. *"Wait isn't that like a hundred years that I spent back in time?"* I said shocked by the number he gave me. *"Actually it's almost 210 years spent back in time. You have even jumped back before you were born, something that I don't recommend you try again."*

Peter words sunk in slowly as I thought about what my life was, but the more I thought about it, the more memories came flooding into my mind about all the things I had gone back in time to change. *"You know Nafisa is a perfect match for you, too bad you have messed with the timeline too much at this point for anything you do to have any kind of effect on the two of you."* Said Peter waving at me as he walked to the door. *"Peter are you up for one last jump to fix every mistake in my life all at once?"* Peter stopped halfway vanished, he turned back to me as his body reappeared.

Chapter 6

Time moves along like a powerful force of nature changing for no man.

No matter how much power we might have, or how much intelligence we possess.

It remains the uncontrollable force just out of our reach of understanding.

But as time rolls along it must submit to fate.

For no matter what time might do even if we find a way to control time itself.

Fate will always play its part and drive us to where we belong even against time itself.

IT WASN'T FATE

"So what do you have in mind?" Peter said staring at me from behind his smile. *"I'll make one slingshot jump starting from early in my life and moving forward through it until I get pulled back to my present. Twenty jumps to change my life, and I know just where to start."* Peter sat in the bed next to me nodding his head. *"I like the sound of that, tell me what do you want from this jump."* I smiled, I only wanted one thing from this jump, and that was to be happy, but I didn't know how I was going to do that. *"Well I want to be free and happy, so let's show time who's the boss shall we."* I replied.

The next day I started planning the jumps, one after the next I made plans, doing research into those days I planned to jump to in order to find the perfect way to change the course of my life. The days passed by slowly as I planned and hid it from Nafisa. Soon those days had turned into two years. At the end of which I was happy to have a plan, but I also knew I was happy because I was with Nafisa. And even though I was happy just spending some of my days with her, I couldn't be satisfied with just that, and I couldn't be happy with the 135 divorces that were floating around in my memories.

"Do you want to get married tomorrow?" I said to Nafisa as we laid on the couch watching TV. I heard her almost choking when I said it. *"Sure, everyone I know already thinks we are anyway so might as well get it over with."* She replied to me. I kissed her lips for the first time as more than a friend, and I knew I wanted the moment to last forever, but of all people, I knew that time stopped for no one.

IT WASN'T FATE

That night as she slept I headed down to the lab. The machines had been running that whole day getting ready for my big jump. *"Are you sure about this?"* Peter said to me from the robot body as we walked up to a metal chair in the center of the lab. *"Yes, I had to make sure I had no regrets before I did this. If everything fails, I'll know the past half-century living my life with her in it was worth it."* I replied to him sitting in the chair and laying back so he could strap me in.

"Remember the first part of the jump will be the hardest, that's when you have to find a way to damage your body without making you sick enough to go to the hospital. Once that's done, the rest will simply be missing a few calls, bus rides, and events. Are you sure you're ready?" I took a deep breath. *"Thanks, Peter, you're the best part of my mind I know of."* I said with a slight laugh, he laughed back and with his huge smile, he spoke the last words before he hit the button. *"Don't you mean I am the best part of you."* He pushed the button and bolts of energy came from every direction all hitting me at the same time.

I was back to when I was sixteen doing some yard work and odd jobs for a neighbor to make money that summer. I looked around at everything that was around me, this couldn't be any worst. I showed up at the one moment I couldn't possibly do anything to cause any kind of damage that wouldn't make me outwardly sick. I looked through everything as fast as I could, I found nothing and I would be jumping any second. Then out of the corner of my eyes, I saw a bottle with pool acid in it. I grabbed it pulled the cap off and squeezed the bottle. A puff of white smoke came from it and went straight into my lungs. I capped the bottle, and I was pulled right from that time.

The next two jumps I was dazed and didn't do what I was supposed to. On the fourth one, I got a hold of myself, at this point, I was already nineteen, and I could still feel the damage that had been done to my lungs. I pulled my phone from my pocket, found Crystal's number, then and sent her a text. **I WANT YOU TO GO, AS LONG AS YOU'RE HAPPY I'M HAPPY TOO.** I hit send and read her reply just before I jumped again. **AWW, I LOVE YOU. I WILL BE BACK ONCE I FINISH MY FIRST SEMESTER.** The next few jumps caught a bit off guard. I had already changed my life enough not to remember what was happening at the time I arrived.

I laid in a hospital bed, without the control of the right half of my body, my phone went off in my lap, it was Kellie. I paused for a moment, but I had to, I picked it up and started talking about her ignoring me while I need her, and by the end of the conversion three minutes later she had stopped talking and told me to leave her alone. A few more jumps of starting fights with her and I found myself on the phone with someone I worked with. I didn't see the name all it said was **work Precious Star**, I started a fight with her the same time. Then hung up on her before the jump was over.

Five more jumps to go and I was starting to lose my self, the strain of moving through time and so far away from where I belonged was beginning to make me forget what I was doing. I came to on the phone with that same person from work the next four jumps, I didn't even have to check because I recognized the voice instantly. Then at the last jump, I was determined to end things with her, and I did end things with her, then told her I never wanted to see her again. Then I hung up.

The call ended and displayed the number and the contact of the call that I just ended, and my heart stopped. It read Nafisa with her Picture and the area code the same as mine. It couldn't be I thought, no I just ended things with the one person I was doing this for. I felt myself begin to be pulled out of the time right as a message from her came through. **DELETE MY NUMBER I NEVER WANT TO SEE YOU AGAIN.**

I snapped back into my body but not where I had left from. It was the place that I had seen before, a world of just colors, no shapes anywhere around me. Everything was gone, nothing was left not even the ground, I floated in the colors as they changed and moved, but at the same time, nothing was changing. I knew what had happened, I had damaged time from all the jumps, and now the universe was falling apart. All because I couldn't just be happy with my life when I had a perfect life already. I floated through this void of nothing and everything for what must have been a millennium, I lost my mind over and over again as I drifted wishing I had never traveled back in time.

Then as if I hit something, I started to fall through the nothingness, I could feel something pulling me. Then pain shot through my whole being then I jumped up screaming. *"Baby what's wrong is something hurting again, or is it too hot."* A voice came from next to me a familiar one, but I couldn't remember where the voice was from or who it belonged to. I looked over to a woman lying next to me looking up at me with a worried look on her face. I knew her but how? It had been so long since I saw a person I had forgotten what they looked like. *"Baby say something are you ok?"* She said as I stayed speechless just staring at her. I was lost, it had been too long I didn't even know if I could still speak at this point.

"Will! What's wrong?" She yelled out jumping up. Her hair fell back it was long and dark with hints of red and purple blended into her hair. She moved, and everything came rushing back, with me dying her hair and her complaining about not wanting me to do it each time then being happy I did it after. *"I'm ok baby I'm sorry I just couldn't think for a minute."* She dropped back down on the bed. *"Lay back down and go to sleep and stop scaring me."* I just smiled and laid down as memories of me and her flooded into my head. I looked down at my hand and saw my ring, it had two words written on it. **LOVE NAFISA.**

The End

"Well, kids what did you think of the story?" I said to my grandkids. "Why do you always put yourself in the story grandpa?" My grandson said, but I was cut off by his sister before I could answer. *"I like grandpas story it was cute he ended up with grandma after all that, but we know it's just a story you were always married to grandma. Mom said you guys lived right next to each other when you were younger. And that's why you guys are always together."* I laughed as they got up and ran off to Nafisa.

I sat smiling for a few minutes as I watched them run to their grandmother. I got up from the chair I was in and walked over to the balcony, I pulled my phone from my pocket and pushed the button on it the screen, it came on, and a hologram of a bunch of things flipped out of it. There in the center was a coin button with the word PETER written under it and a blue circle just under the coin. I pushed it, and a five-inch circle was projected in front of me, then it just started changing colors. *"I shouldn't expect you to work again, but I was hoping you had some life left in you."* I said tapping the phone then closing it.

I walked back to the chair I was in earlier and sat in it holding my phone in my hand. **BEEP.** The phone beeped in my hand, I looked down and opened it. *"Peter. Personal enquiry time evaluation and rest interface, now online. What may I help you with today, sir."* I just laughed. *"Ah, I don't know what I expected after all this time."* I said as

IT WASN'T FATE

I closed the phone and put it on the table. *"P...p...peter is on... line line line."* It said again, I looked over at it on the table, and laughed louder. *"Did I really expect you to be Peter, man I must be losing it if I thought this computer was going to be my lost hallucination."* I said laughing to myself.

"You always thought too highly of yourself Will." I stopped laughing as a projection of Peter appeared over the phone. *"No way this can't be you don't exist here."* I said as I took a closer look at it. *"Ha you are clueless, I was never part of your mind from the time I became Peter. You don't remember, but you wrote me as an AI when you first discovered time travel so long ago. My job was to try and keep you from destroying the universe and time itself, and reset the timeline in case something went wrong I am in a sense the ultimate failsafe for time travelers to ensure time doesn't get damaged too badly. I can also seal all of the holes you have punched through time, but if I do that you can no longer travel through time, but it also means that the damage you caused will be healed."* It said to me.

I looked up at my family and the little ones running around with a smile. *"Seal it, I don't want to ever lose this no matter what happens next after all I did do a lot to get to this point."* I said with a smile. Peters face turned into a smile, the one I had missed seeing every day. *"I thought you would say that oh and one last thing, I had to reset your jumps right after you got your so sick otherwise you would've destroyed all of time. So it turns out you had nothing to do with this. I guess this was what fate had in mind all along."* He said then vanished as the phone went dead.

Chapter 7

With each passing day time is molded by fate.

Fate is molded by the choices we make.

So never look back to the past trying to change what has already happened.

Instead look forward to what you want and create your own fate.

Create a tomorrow you can hold on to and look back on with no regrets.

IT WASN'T FATE

I walked over to Nafisa as she played with the grandkids. I looked at her as she laughed with the kids. Then pulled a keychain from my pocket that I had made for us over a century ago when we first met. I held it up and looked at it as I did many times before thinking about the past. What was, what could have been, and what I had changed or at least thought I had changed. As I thought I looked at the keychain and the picture on it, and something strange happened. I saw writing on it that I had never seen before, it was engraved in Nafisa handwriting. I held it closer so I could read what it said, it was in letters that seem to glow and shimmer changing almost writing itself as I started to read it. What it said brought back a flood of memories of the life me and her had shared over the past centuries. Those three words that stuck with me from the beginning of our relationship until now. Carrying with it all the love we felt for each other.

Until Forever Dies

Time is only an illusion

Thank you for coming on this wondrous
adventure with me.
I hope you enjoyed reading it as much as
I enjoyed writing it.

Cursed Heroes book series
Ten Thousand Walks: A Legend Is Born
Print: 978-1-7359149-1-6
Ebook: 978-1-7359149-0-9
Loaded
Ebook: 978-1-7359149-2-3
Print: 978-1-7359149-3-0
Cold As Ice
Ebook: 978-1-7359149-4-7
Print: 978-1-7359149-5-4
Other Books available at: Mowuniverse.
com/store
See you in the next adventure

www.ingramcontent.com/pod-product-compliance
Lightning Source LLC
Chambersburg PA
CBHW070115260626
47160CB00004B/1485